*A figure emerged from the truck. Even through the heavy gray mist that enveloped him, Quinn could see the flaming carrot-red hair and his sparkling blue eyes.*

*"Hello there!" he called. "You lost?"*

*"Yes. I guess so."*

*"Where you going?" The young man hopped off the running board and came toward her.*

*"My dad's." Then she realized she hadn't said who her dad was. "David Philips. He just married Beverly Harris. I'm going to spend the summer with them."*

*"Are you?" He smiled. "I'm Logan James, by the way." He extended a hand. "Funny, neither Ben nor Beverly mentioned you."*

*"You know them?"*

*Logan grinned. "Sure I do. Everyone knows the Harris house." His grin faded. "And about Ben's exploits," he added almost under his breath.*

Dear Readers:

Thank you for your unflagging interest in First Love From Silhouette. Your many helpful letters have shown us that you have appreciated growing and stretching with us, and that you demand more from your reading than happy endings and conventional love stories. In the months to come we will make sure that our stories go on providing the variety you have come to expect from us. We think you will enjoy our unusual plot twists and unpredictable characters who will surprise and delight you without straying too far from the concerns that are very much part of all our daily lives.

We hope you will continue to share with us your ideas about how to keep our books your very First Loves. We depend on you to keep us on our toes!

Nancy Jackson
Senior Editor
FIRST LOVE FROM SILHOUETTE

# A GATHERING STORM
## Serita Stevens

*First Love from Silhouette*
Published by Silhouette Books New York
**America's Publisher of Contemporary Romance**

**SILHOUETTE BOOKS**
300 E. 42nd St., New York, N.Y.  10017

Copyright © 1986 by Serita Deborah Stevens

ISBN: 0-373-06190-0

First Silhouette Books printing June 1986

America's Publisher of Contemporary Romance

Printed in the U.S.A.

RL 5.5, IL age 11 and up

**SERITA STEVENS** teaches college-level writing, and is the author of seven novels and a number of television and radio scripts. A graduate of the University of Illinois, she has also trained as nurse. Her interests include horseback riding and flying planes.

# Chapter One

Quinn Philips bit into a chocolate graham cracker. Hearing the door close below, she sat up quickly, shoved the box of snacks and the novel under her bed and turned the radio off. She pulled out her biology text and pretended intense concentration just as her mother opened the door.

"Studying for your finals, honey?"

Quinn nodded. Brushing her dark, curly hair out of her eyes, she tried to ignore Alexander the Great, her black cat. The half-

Siamese jumped up on her shoulders and began licking the cracker crumbs from Quinn's face.

"Stop it!" Quinn said, watching her mother put away the laundry.

Alex jumped down and landed lightly on the floor. Meowing, lifting himself up on his hind paws, he begged Quinn for more of her treat.

"Get away," she commanded.

Undaunted, the cat scooted under the bed and pushed out the nearly empty box of chocolate grahams.

"Alex," Quinn warned, but it was too late. Her mother had already turned around.

"Oh, Quinn!" Mrs. Philips grabbed the box off the floor. "You've eaten practically the whole box."

"I was hungry." She shrugged and put down her book.

"Quinn, you know you have to watch yourself. The pink dress barely fits you. With the wedding in two weeks, there isn't much time for further alterations."

Quinn glared mutinously at her mother. She didn't like Mom trying to control her eating habits, even though she knew her mother was probably right. She did have to watch herself. Not that she was really overweight, but she could easily lose five pounds. If only she could lose those blasted freckles, as well. They made her look so childish.

"I trust that your eating won't be a problem when you go to your father's this summer."

"Oh, Mom, come on. Can't I stay here? I can take care of myself. After all, I am sixteen. Don't you trust me?"

"Quinn, we've been through this several times already. You know trust is not the issue. Honey, you haven't seen your father since Christmas. I don't think I could really enjoy my honeymoon with Paul knowing you'd be alone. What if something happened?"

"Nothing's going to happen. Besides, I could always go to Jen's or Cathy's."

"Darling, your father wants to see you. He wants to get to know you better."

"Well if he wanted to get to know me he didn't have to leave us."

"Quinn, baby, your father does care about you. Really, he does."

"Mom, please, don't make me go there for the whole summer! I won't have any of my friends."

"You'll have Ben, your new stepbrother."

Quinn made a face. "He's twenty-one, Mom. He probably thinks I'm a baby. Can't I at least come home after the six weeks when you and Paul return from England? I just know I won't be able to get along with Dad for the whole summer! Don't you remember all the fights we used to have? Besides—" she swallowed hard "—I don't think I could even be pleasant to *her*. Let me stay at Cathy's. Please?"

"Quinn, don't be like this."

She knew she was fighting a losing battle and it simply wasn't fair. Why did parents always have to have their way?

"Listen, I promise I'll call you at Dave's just as soon as I return from Europe. If it's really that bad, I'll let you come home."

"All right." Quinn sighed. Then she glanced at Alex, who had jumped up on the bed again.

"All right, I'll go for the six weeks, but only if you let me take Alex with me!"

"I suppose it's 'all right.'" Her mother's tone was doubtful. "I'll have to ask your father."

Her mother's wedding was beautiful—although Quinn hadn't expected anything less. Still, it brought tears to her eyes, seeing the way Mom looked at Paul and the way Paul looked at Mom. Quinn felt like disappearing into a wall. For all the attention anyone paid her, she might as well have. Not that she didn't want her mother to be happy—she truly did. She liked Paul Elliot, too. She clutched the flowers and watched the ceremony.

Why couldn't her father have stayed? Why did he have to go fall in love with some secretary in Boston? That wasn't supposed to happen. Love was supposed to be for keeps. Love was forever.

"You look beautiful," Paul told her later, handing her some champagne, her first champagne, in the toast to the new couple.

"Thanks," Quinn replied. She didn't feel so beautiful. Mom had been right. Her dress was a tad too tight. She shouldn't have indulged in all those chocolate grahams. She longed for the ceremony to be over so she could change to her jeans and blouson top for the trip.

"Come on, Sweetie, smile," Paul coaxed. "You're supposed to be happy."

"I am," Quinn said. "Can't you tell? I'm jumping for joy."

Paul brushed back one of Quinn's reckless dark curls that had defied the thick layer of hair spray. "Your mother told me that you're not keen about being with your father for the summer."

"I told you, I'm wild with happiness."

"You'll have to give him a chance—sooner or later."

"I'd rather it was later."

Paul was silent.

"Maybe you'll meet someone nice out on the Cape. Maybe your new stepbrother will introduce you to some of his friends."

"I doubt it. He probably won't want me hanging about. Besides, who'd want me?"

Paul's brown eyes took on a mischievous glint. "Well, actually, I overheard something about a Justin Connor..."

Quinn drew in her breath sharply. "What do you mean?"

Her mom came up and Quinn forced herself to be silent.

"What are you two gossiping about?"

"I'll tell you later, Quinn," Paul said, winking at his stepdaughter and walking away.

Could it be true? Justin Connor was only the most popular boy in her junior class. Paul had to be lying! If he wasn't, it made things all the worse. Quinn was sure that by the time she returned to Evanston, Justin would be hooked by Amelia, Susan or one of the other popular girls.

"You know your plane leaves at five tonight. Are you all packed?" her mother asked.

"Yes," Quinn said. "Everything's done except for Alex. I think I'd better take some extra food for him and some litter—just in case Dad can't get any so late."

"Good idea. I'll see you back at the house then, darling."

Quinn watched as her mother melted into the crowd of well-wishers. Feeling sad and abandoned, she picked up one of the chocolate cream cakes—her favorite—and stuffed the whole thing into her mouth. She was going to hate the summer at her father's—she knew it.

O'Hare was busy, as usual. Mom stood with Quinn at the counter. Their flights left exactly fifteen minutes apart, only Mom and Paul weren't going to Boston. Their flight was to New York, where they would catch the night plane to Paris.

"You're sure you'll be all right, Quinn? I still think that Dave should have come for you himself."

"Oh, Mother! It's not as if I haven't flown before."

The new Mrs. Elliot frowned.

"Really, Mom, I'll be okay." A twitch came to Quinn's lips. "Of course, if you really don't like it, I can always stay home with Cathy."

"Quinn, baby, you know I can't do that." She kissed her daughter as the plane to Boston was called. "I wish I could give you the address of where we'll be, but you can always call Gram during the next few weeks if any problems come up.''

''If anything comes up,'' Quinn said stiffly, ''I'll handle it myself.''

Mother glanced toward the tunnel entrance of the plane. Nearly everyone had boarded. ''What do you want me to bring you?''

''A Greek god.''

''How about some Greek sandals instead?'' Her mom touched Quinn's cheek gently. ''You've got enough time to worry about Greek gods when you get older.''

Quinn shrugged. That was the trouble with being sixteen. She was too old for some things and not old enough for others. She hated being in between.

''Kiss me goodbye, Quinn?''

Quinn swallowed the sadness in her. Putting down her case, she embraced her mother. ''Have a good time, Mom,'' Quinn whispered, ''and don't forget about me.''

''Sweetheart, how could I forget about you? Believe me, you'll enjoy being with Dad this summer. I wouldn't be doing it if I didn't think it was the best for you.''

"Yeah.'' Quinn gave an exaggerated sigh. "I know, Mom. I just want to be treated like an adult already. I hate all this coddling.''

"Believe me, Quinn, when you're an adult, you won't want to be. Enjoy being young while you can.''

Quinn picked up the case and started toward the waiting stewardess.

"Quinn?''

She turned once more.

"Give my best to your father.'' Mrs. Elliot's voice choked.

"Yeah, Mom, I will.''

"And be nice to Beverly. Listen to what she says, clean up your room and do the dishes. Or at least offer.''

"Yeah, Mom, I will.''

Picking up her case for the last time, Quinn hurried onto the plane and found her seat.

She had hoped she would get put next to a good-looking guy, but that only happened in romance novels—not in real life, she decided when she spotted her seat partner—an elderly lady.

Quinn took out her sketch pad. She wasn't any great shakes in art, but it was fun. Actually, Quinn's best subjects were chemistry and biology—in spite of her current dislike of the teacher they had. Ever since she had rescued Alexander the Great, she had wanted to become a doctor, or maybe a vet. She wasn't sure yet. She liked animals almost as much as she liked people . . . and they didn't betray her love the way her father had.

Trying to hide her emotions, Quinn sketched furiously with her soft pencil. It was a picture of Alexander and quite a good likeness, even if she said so herself.

She closed her eyes. She wondered what Beverly would be like, and more important, what Ben was like. She hoped Paul was right. Maybe despite their age difference, they would become friends. Maybe he'd even have some younger friends—friends that he could introduce Quinn to. Maybe the summer wouldn't be totally wasted.

It would be neat if she could come home and tell Cathy and Jen that she had a boyfriend. Just thinking about that helped Quinn to refuse the layer cake the stewardess offered her for dessert. She wouldn't just lose five pounds, she would lose ten and then she would be like the ugly duckling turning into a swan.

Absorbed in her thoughts, she scarcely noticed the thunder and lightning outside. Not until the flashing sign for seat belts told her that they were nearing Boston did Quinn even realize that the plane was rocking slightly. Her heart hammered. Would her dad be waiting for her at the airport? Hadn't he promised Mom he would be?

What would she say to him and what would he say to her?

Pressing her lips together, Quinn tried to quell the feeling that everything wasn't as perfect as her mother wanted it to be.

"Don't be silly," she told herself. It was just nerves. As long as she had been forced to come, Quinn decided she would make the best of it, even if Ben was as stuckup as she thought he might be. Her father was her father, no matter what.

The pilot's voice came over the loudspeaker just as the lightning flashed in front of Quinn's eyes. She shivered watching the white electrical storm jag across the black sky like a silver knife cutting chocolate cake. As instructed, she buckled her seat belt.

An hour later the United jet touched down at Logan Airport. Quinn glanced around the terminal. Where was Dad? Surely the fact that the plane was a little late couldn't have put him off. After all, he could easily have checked with the desk.

Puzzled, she went to collect her luggage and Alex.

The cat mewed delightedly when he saw her and begged to be let out of his cardboard carrier.

"Not yet, Alexander. We're not at Dad's yet."

Alex continued his loud crying as Quinn glanced about again. Could Dad have forgotten her, after all the promises he had made to Mom?

Yes, it was all too possible for Dad to have forgotten her. Hadn't he forgotten her by coming out here to marry Beverly Harris? Besides, he had always been one of those absent-minded professors. If you didn't constantly remind Dad about a job, then it was usually forgotten. She put her hand inside the case to comfort Alex. If only she had someone to comfort and hug her, too.

Her eyes continued to scan the airport. People milled about the luggage area; people greeted one another but none of the people were her father.

She supposed that the most logical thing to do would be to phone him. Digging into her purse for the Cape Cod phone number that Mom had given her, she went to the phones.

Good. It was ringing. Soon her dad would answer and would laughingly excuse himself for not being there. But there was no answer. Just as she was about to hang up, a woman's voice came on.

"Bev... Beverly?" Quinn asked.

"This is Boston special operator number two. What number did you want?"

"Oh," Quinn felt deflated. "I wanted 555-2246."

"Just a moment," the woman said in a singsong voice. "It seems as if the number is temporarily disconnected."

Disconnected? Quinn's mouth went dry. "Isn't, isn't there some other number I can call? Maybe you could check if you have the right number of David Philips, just outside of Woods Hole."

The operator paused a moment. "That number is correct. I'm sorry, but the line is out of order."

"Oh," Quinn stared into the phone. "Thanks." She replaced the receiver. It seemed as if the whole world was conspiring against her. What could she do now?

"Well, Alex—" she bent to talk to the cat "—what do you want to do? Spend the night in the airport and go home in the morning? Mom would be awfully angry if we did that, though."

The cat cried out his agreement, pawing the cage once more as he asked to be let out. Suddenly he arched his back and hissed.

"Oh, Alex, don't you give me problems, too." The cat continued to hiss and Quinn glanced up. She was aware now of being watched by a tall, lanky man lounging against one of the white posts.

She felt a sinking sensation in her stomach. Weren't there kidnappers and con men who haunted airports looking for runaways and young girls alone?

She picked Alex up and hurried back to the luggage carousel where her bags lay. Even there people were rapidly leaving. She glanced nervously about. The man was still lounging against the post, watching her from under heavy lids, as if he were assessing her as a potential victim.

Quinn scanned the terminal once more.

She was so worried that she barely heard her name being called over the loudspeaker. Dad! Dad was here after all! In a rush of hope, she grabbed Alex's box and hurried over to the white page phone.

"This is Quinn Philips," she said, excited and brushing her unruly curls from her face. "Is my father—"

"I have a message for you, Miss Philips," the operator interrupted in a nasal tone.

"A message?"

"It's from a David Philips. He says he's sorry he can't pick you up today. He wants you to take the bus to the terminal in Falmouth. Your stepbrother will meet you there, he says."

"Oh." Quinn found herself glancing toward the pillar where the strange man had been lounging. She was relieved that he had disappeared.

"Do you need me to repeat that?"

"No. How do I get to the buses?" How would she ever manage alone with her two cases, her purse and Alex?

"Taxi would be best. You have to go into the city for that."

"Great. Thanks," and hung up. She should have expected this kind of treatment from her father. If he really cared about her, he would have come to fetch her himself. No, if he really loved her, if he really cared, he wouldn't have left them in the first place.

Glancing around, she reassured herself that the fellow who had been staring at her had gone.

"Okay, Alex," she said to the crying cat as she lifted the cases, putting the smaller one under her arm and hooking the handle of larger one in her right hand, "let's go." It wasn't the easiest way to move or the fastest, but yes, she could manage. In fact, Dad or not, Quinn was sure she could manage whatever the summer had in store.

# Chapter Two

The bus trip took longer than Quinn expected. With an aching head, she leaned against the window. There weren't many passengers in this bus. It was the last run of the evening. She had been lucky to reach the station just five minutes before the Greyhound pulled out.

Worse, she couldn't even see anything. The thunder and lightning, which had delayed their landing, now prevented Quinn from viewing the scenery as the bus rolled toward the Cape. Everything was shrouded in fog.

Her stomach tightened. She didn't like not being able to see where she was, but at least she didn't have to do the driving. She patted her wallet. Just last week, before school had ended, Quinn had received her student driver's permit. Soon Mom would be letting her use the car. Maybe she could get Dad to let her practice this summer.

She leaned against the window again, lulled by the steady sound of the rain.

She realized she had dozed when the bus rolled to a stop. Glancing about the vehicle, she saw the driver coming toward her. Rubbing her eyes, she tried to get her bearings. The countryside was still blanketed with a thick mist and streetlights glowed with an eerie halo. She shivered, feeling the dampness penetrating her bones. She was still dazed from her nap.

"You wanted Woods Hole, Miss?"

"Yes . . . I . . ."

"Well, here it is."

Without recalling that the message had told her to go to Falmouth terminal, Quinn nodded and stood up. She picked up Alexander and his carrier from the seat next to her and grabbed her purse.

Only as the driver put her two cases on the damp ground and she felt the drizzle hit her face did Quinn realize her mistake. But it was too late. The bus was already moving away.

"Oh, Alex," she said to the cat, "what do I do now? Dad's phone is out of order and Ben is probably waiting for me at the Falmouth terminal. I'll bet he'll be furious that I'm not there! I wonder how far Falmouth terminal is?"

The cat scratched at his carrier and stuck out a black paw, demanding to be let out and crying for his mistress's attention. Quinn sighed and straightened. She could feel the rain on her cheek. She was sure Mom had packed her raincoat, but it didn't do her any good hidden in the suitcase.

She grimaced and looked down the long, lonely road. Was this the famous Route 6? No, it just couldn't be the main road of the Cape.

"This is just great, Quinn Catherine Philips," she told herself. "You don't know where you are, and you can't even call since Dad's phone is out of order." She felt tired and achy from the plane and bus. She wanted to go back to sleep, but most of all, Quinn wanted her dad. It was childish, she knew, but she didn't feel very adult at this moment.

Alexander began to mew. Well, there didn't seem any point in just standing there. She picked up her cases as she had at the airport and began to trudge forward in the muddy rain, forward to the lights. Maybe someone would give her shelter and they would be able to contact her father.

She was so lost in her new misery and thoughts of her father that she scarcely heard the battered pickup truck as it came rumbling down the road. It wasn't until the vehicle stopped and the headlights beamed directly on her that Quinn actually paused.

A figure emerged from the truck. Even through the heavy fog that enveloped them, Quinn could see his flaming, carrot-red hair and sparkling blue eyes.

"Hello, there!" he called. "You lost?"

"Yes. I guess so."

"Where you going?" The young man hopped off the runningboard and came toward her.

"My dad's." Then she realized he wouldn't know who her father was. "David Philips. He . . . he just married Beverly Harris. I'm supposed to spend the summer with them."

"Are you?" He smiled. "I'm Logan James, by the way." He extended a hand. "Funny, neither Ben nor Beverly mentioned you."

"You know them?"

Logan grinned. "Sure. Everyone knows the Harris house." His grin faded, "And about Ben's exploits," he added almost under his breath.

"Exploits?"

"Never mind. Was someone supposed to meet you . . . ?"

"Quinn. Quinn's my name. Uh, yes. Someone, my stepbrother, was supposed to meet the bus."

Logan frowned.

"But it's not his fault he's not here. I made the mistake. I told the driver I was going to Woods Hole. I forgot that the message at the airport said I should take the bus to Falmouth."

"I see."

Quinn wasn't sure what Logan was seeing, but she knew that he was eyeing her bedraggled appearance. How awful she must look.

"Well, you'd better not wait out in this rain." He picked up her case. "Can you manage the rest?"

Quinn nodded.

"Good. I'll drive you to your dad's. The Harris house isn't much farther down the road."

"Oh. Oh, thanks," Quinn said, picking up Alex's case.

As she slid into the truck, he took the carrier from her. "Does he have a name?"

"Of course. Alexander the Great."

"Good name for a half-Siamese."

"How did you know he's half-Siamese?"

"Not too many black Siamese, but his cry gives him away."

Quinn nodded. "You're an animal person, too."

"You could say that. I plan to be a vet."

"Oh. So do I. Well, I'm not sure if I'll be a vet or a regular doctor." She sneezed hard.

"Well, unless we get you into a warm house and dry clothes, you're not going to be anything." He started the truck and turned it around on the dark road.

"You're here for the whole summer?"

"Yes. My mother's gotten married again and gone on her honeymoon. I was sent here."

She hadn't realized the hurt that was in her voice, but it must have been obvious to Logan, for his hand brushed hers briefly. "You must be feeling pretty terrible, what with your mom leaving and your new stepbrother not picking you up."

"It's not Ben's fault. I mean, my dad was supposed to meet me at the airport and he couldn't. I fouled up the message by getting off at the wrong place. It's my fault, not his."

"Nevertheless, it must be kind of tough."

"No," she said finally. Her voice was tight. "I'm okay. I have Alexander."

Logan gave a brief glance at the cat still pawing and crying as he tried to get out of the cage.

"Yeah, maybe, but sometimes you need people, too. Ben tends to get rather wrapped up in himself." His hand touched her shoulder, and it was all Quinn could do to keep the tears controlled. "If you need to talk to anyone this summer, I'd be happy to lend an ear."

He paused a moment more and braked the truck just as a low sports car came roaring down the road. Even with the mist, she could see the car fast approaching them in the rearview mirror, the lights glaring as if the driver owned the road.

"Well, what do you know? If it isn't the devil himself."

"Who?"

"Your stepbrother, Ben Harris." Logan honked to draw attention to them.

The car in front of them continued forward at a furious pace, and the rev of its motor could be heard over the thunder, wind and crashing waves.

"He's not stopping."

"So I see." Logan grimaced. Without another word, he turned the pickup across the road so that it obstructed both lanes.

"Logan—" Quinn remonstrated.

"Don't worry. He'll stop."

The red Porsche came to a screeching halt inches from the passenger side.

"James! What the...?" A dark-haired, immaculately dressed man stepped from the car, slamming the door behind him.

"Be quiet, Ben. I had good reasons. You weren't going to stop—"

"No, I wasn't going to stop. I have nothing to say to you or your family."

"Maybe not, but you have something to say to her. Quinn?" He extended his hand and Quinn took it, easing herself out of Logan's side of the truck, since her side was blocked.

"Ben Harris, may I present your new stepsister, Quinn Philips."

Ben's mouth dropped slightly, and then recovering, he glared at her. "You were supposed to be at Falmouth."

"I know but I—"

"It doesn't matter where she was supposed to be. She's here now. Actually her father was supposed to pick her up at the airport."

"That's not my fault," Ben said. Even from where she stood, Quinn could see the redness of his eyes. Had he been drinking? "I just got the call from Dave to go get her. He had forgotten to tell me."

Quinn stiffened. Wasn't that just like her father—to make plans involving someone else and then not let them know until the last minute.

"Wait a second. How could he have called you? I tried earlier from the airport. They told me that the line was disconnected."

Ben flushed. "It wasn't disconnected. It was out of order with the storm. Anyway, I don't think he was calling from home."

"Oh," Quinn said.

Logan glanced at her and then at Ben. "I don't think your sister should be out anymore in this rain." He leaned into the truck and brought out her suitcases.

"What's that?" Ben motioned to Alex's carrier.

"My cat."

"Does Mom know you've got a cat?"

Quinn glared at him. "She should. Dad was told."

"All right. Get in. I'll take you up to the house."

Logan stepped up to her door as Ben got into his side. "I'm on the beach a lot or in the phone directory," he said to Quinn.

"Thanks," she said awkwardly.

"You finished, Logan James?" Ben asked impatiently.

"For now." Logan stepped away from the car as Ben pressed the button that electronically closed the window.

The car went into sharp reverse and spun around. Quinn saw that Logan didn't move the truck until she was out of sight.

She glanced at the speedometer. "Shouldn't you be going just a little slower?"

Ben glared at her. "Listen, Quinn, I grew up on these roads. No one else knows them better than I do. Nobody forced you to ride with me, you know."

Quinn kept quiet, fighting the response. She could tell this was not going to be the easy relationship that Paul had envisioned, but she had promised her mom she would be nice.

As Ben pressed the accelerator once more, Alex began to hiss.

"You'd better watch that cat of yours. I don't like cats and neither does my mother." Ben said. "I'm sure your father didn't tell her or she would have forbidden it."

"Well, if he didn't tell her," Quinn said, "that's not my fault. I'll keep him in my room."

"You do that," Ben responded as Alex arched his back and hissed once more. "And tell him not to make that awful noise. I don't like it. Makes me nervous."

"Cat's don't take orders the way dogs do." She put her hand into the carrier to stroke Alex's furry head. She didn't understand why Alex was acting this way. He was usually such a friendly cat. Probably he was as exhausted from the trip as she was. Maybe he sensed Ben's disapproval. With his wide green eyes,

Alex stared up at her, begging again as his paw touched her face to be let out.

"Soon, honey, soon," Quinn whispered. She could feel Ben's eyes on her, but what did she care what he thought?

It was several minutes more before they reached the Harris house on its isolated strip of beach.

The house was illuminated from behind by the lightning. It looked desolate. The thick mist rising from the sea added to the gloom. Quinn glanced at Ben. This couldn't be where he lived, where Dad lived, and where she would be for the summer!

Ben noticed her silence. "A beauty, isn't it? The family albatross."

"You don't like it?"

"I could think of better ways to spend the money. I'd much rather have a town apartment in Boston, but Mother'll never sell. It's been in the family for generations and now that your father is here..."

Quinn gave him a sharp look. The way Ben had said "your father" seemed abrupt. Didn't he like her dad? She wanted to ask him, but now was not the time.

"I bet it has a fascinating history to it."

"Sure it does. Spooks, Underground Railroad, the works. Built in the early 1800s by one Jeremiah Harris. Mom'll tell you all about it, I'm sure."

"Looks pretty spooky now," Quinn commented. Even as she spoke, the lightning flashed again and she felt her muscles contract.

"Well, it's not haunted." Ben gave her a sour laugh. "I can assure you of that." After he had parked he began to lift her cases from the car. "You take the cat."

Quinn picked up Alex's carrier. "It's okay, boy. We're almost there."

Thunder rumbled. Quinn jumped as Ben called from the now-open front door. "Well, come on, kid. I haven't got all day."

Stifling her angry retort, Quinn hurried after him into the house. The slamming of the screen door behind her had an ominous finality. She squinted, seeing the shadows playing on the walls and the long row of portraits in the hall. "Ben?" He couldn't have deserted her! She called again.

"Up here." He leaned over the banister, his shadow looming against the wall behind him.

"Oh." She let a sigh of relief escape. "Can you put on a light?"

"Can't. Storm blew it out. I'll get a candle if you need one."

"No, I can manage." Quinn put her hand on the smooth wood of the rail and edged up, carrying Alex and her smaller case.

The Harris house was a colonial salt box—square and massive—but over the years additions and changes had been made. Now there was a porch with a swing and a balcony off the master bedroom, as well as what appeared to be a widow's walk on top of the house. At least, Quinn thought, as she reached the landing and followed Ben's voice up the faded carpet of the staircase, she'd have something of interest to explore on rainy days. Maybe she could even sketch a picture of it.

Ben threw open a door on the corner of the second floor. "Here." He put her case inside. "This is yours. Bathroom's there." He pointed to the tiled room illuminated by the occasional flashes of lightning. She nodded as the shrill of the phone pierced the silence about them.

"It's working."

"So I see." Ben disappeared to answer it. She could hear him mumbling as she followed him down the hall.

"No, I know," he said. "She didn't get there." He paused. Quinn wondered whom he was talking to. "She's here." His back was to her, and obviously he didn't know she was in the room with him. "We'll take care of that matter another time."

A roll of thunder reverberated through the house. Suddenly the rooms were flooded with light. Electricity had returned.

"I'll talk to you later," Ben said to the person calling and quickly hung up. He turned and saw Quinn. "I thought you were waiting for me in your room."

"I was," Quinn said, "but I . . . was curious."

"Curiosity killed the cat."

"Was that my father on the phone?"

"Nope."

"Where are my father and Beverly?"

"Some political meeting. Beverly's all involved with the local community rot. That's why they couldn't pick you up."

"Oh." A political meeting was more important to Dad than she was. It figured.

"Why do you call her Beverly? Isn't she your real mother?"

"Yeah, she's my real mother. But Beverly's her name." His smile was more like a jagged line cut on his face. "Come on. I'll get you some towels."

He led the way out of the room and back to where Quinn's things were.

"Here you are. Wash your face. You look a sight. Didn't your mother ever tell you not to rub your eyes when you have makeup on?"

"Thanks for the compliment—and the towels. I think I'll wash up and get to bed."

"Suit yourself." Ben shrugged. He turned on his heel and slammed the door to her room behind him.

She stared at the closed door until Alex's mewing reminded her that he was still in his carrier. Leaning down, she undid the latch.

"Hello, there. You're a good boy."

Grateful for the freedom, Alex began to explore his new quarters, sniffing at the floor, the braided rug and the bed. He jumped onto the blue velvet Queen Anne chair and then lightly onto the ruffled spread on the canopy bed. Mewing with pleasure, he hopped over to the Sheraton writing table and chair where he began to scratch.

"No!" Quinn yelled. "Bad, Alex." She took him back to the bed. "Bed, chair or floor only. I don't want Beverly forcing you out."

Alex glared at her but complied as he settled like a furry ball into the Queen Anne chair's soft fabric.

Satisfied that he was all right, Quinn went to wash. Ben had been right. She was a mess. Had Logan thought that, too? Why was it she always looked her worst when she met cute guys?

She heard the sound of a car below. Was Dad back? She leaned down but couldn't see anything. Then out of the corner of her eye, she saw the red Porsche appear at the edge of the road. Ben was driving off again. He had left her alone in the big house. Her stomach rumbled, but she wasn't about to go to the kitchen herself, not when fingers of mist stretched like a vise around the house.

The canopy bed looked inviting. She crawled in under the covers. Outside, the thunder clapped and the wind howled. Feeling very much alone, she pulled the covers over her head and tried not to listen to the sounds of the storm.

# Chapter Three

Huddling in bed, Quinn stared up at the shadows on the canopy and listened to the unfamiliar sounds of the house. She could hear Alex exploring the room—jumping lightly from the chair to the dresser and back before he decided on the bed. The springs creaked.

"Will you please settle down?"

His ears went up. He looked at her with such a pathetic wide-eyed stare that Quinn immediately felt remorse for her sharp tone. "Come here, baby." She patted the bed next to her.

The cat started forward. His black coat was in striking contrast to the whiteness of the canopy and the bedspread. He was halfway across to her when a flash of lightning illuminated the room. Alex sprang off the mattress and dived under the chair.

"Don't be such a chicken," Quinn gently scolded him, "Come on back." Once more she patted the space beside her. It took a few minutes more before Alexander decided that the storm wasn't going to bother him and returned to the bed.

"Not at my feet. Up here." He stared at her a moment and then gingerly started forward.

Quinn lifted her covers and Alex peered under. She touched his soft fur and stroked his neck. "You're the only one who loves me, Alex. Not even Daddy loves me. Otherwise he would have picked me up."

She watched him a few minutes before closing her eyes, but even then sleep did not come quickly. Exhausted from her trip as she was, she couldn't help wondering what this summer was going to bring. Had her mom been right? Would she and her father become closer? Or would she just grow to hate him even more?

Wind moved through the old house on ghostly steps, and the rafters creaked. She thought she heard someone in the house. But that was just her overactive imagination, wasn't it? Maybe there were mice? Alex would be happy about that. Quinn recalled the one time Alex had proudly brought a dead mouse to her. He was such a smart cat. Somehow Alex had known it was her birthday—her father hadn't.

The rain continued to tap at the window like Morse code. Was someone sending a message for help in the storm? The idea was so ridiculous that she almost giggled in relief. Aware of Alex's steady breathing as he cuddled at her side, she touched him again. She wanted to fall asleep, but she couldn't. All her nerves seemed alive as she listened to the sounds and smelled the ocean breeze coming in. Would her father get home before she fell asleep? Did he even care that she was here? Tomorrow, she would talk to him. Maybe tomorrow she would see Logan James again, too.

Her hand resting on Alex, she fell into a light sleep.

Quinn knew she had to be dreaming because she was wearing the pink chiffon dress she had worn at Mom's wedding—and she was running on the beach. She heard sounds, like doors closing, but there were no doors in her dream. Narrowing her eyes, she looked up to the house perched on the cliff and realized it was the Harris house.

In the top windows, lights were on. They looked like eyes—staring at her. Whichever way she ran, the lighted eyes chased her. There was someone or something chasing her, but she couldn't see what.

Breathless, she continued along the beach. Her feet sank deeper and deeper into the wet sand as she looked for a place to hide. There was laughter coming from the house. The door, like a mouth, had opened.

Not watching her path, she felt herself tripping on something and heard a cry. As Quinn looked down, the object that had caused her fall was a dead cat—Alexander! The cat's body was stiff like a board and crusted with blood. Quinn screamed.

Rainwater was hitting her face. She cried out again.

The noise, enough to wake her, made Quinn realize that the rainwater was only Alex washing her face with his scratchy tongue.

Seeing she was awake, he jumped off the bed and ran to the door. He began pawing at it and mewing. He turned to her expectantly, but she didn't move from the bed. Persistently, he returned to nudge her. He licked her eyes, her cheek and urged her to follow him. "You naughty boy! What do you want?"

Quinn looked at her open window. The dark sky told her day was several hours off. He couldn't be hungry. His bowl still had food in it. "What's wrong, Alex? Has the storm upset you?" She looked into his saucer-green eyes illuminated by the flash of the lightning.

A footboard in the room creaked. Quinn caught her breath and peered into the darkness around her. She couldn't see anything. She was sure it was only her imagination, but nevertheless, she asked, "Hello? Is someone there?"

She strained her eyes again, but could still see nothing. She shivered. "Come on, boy." She patted the bed. "Let's go back to sleep."

Alex refused to obey. He continued to paw at the door and cry.

Quinn kicked off her blankets and left her warm bed, prepared to scoop him up, only to stop halfway. The door to her room, was open a crack. She stared at the handle. She was sure she had locked it before going to sleep. She recalled turning the bolt. A cold chill ran through her.

"Okay. It's still night, Alex. I'm locking this door for sure this time, and then I'm going to sleep." She said, willing herself to get out of bed and slide the bolt.

She scurried back across the threadbare carpet and threw herself into bed, pulling the covers over her head. Nearly a half hour later, she was awakened again. Peering out from under the covers, she was horrified to see the door handle move ever so lightly. She hadn't heard anyone enter the house. The handle continued to turn. Quinn sat up on her elbows. "Hello? Hello, who's there?" she called. Maybe her dad had come back and wanted to say goodnight?

Throwing back the covers, she hurried over to the door and unlocked it. No one there. Flashes of lightning, remnants of the dying storm sporadically lit the halls, illuminating the portraits of long-dead ancestors.

Alex followed her out, rubbing at her ankles.

Someone had tried to come into the room. But who?

Throwing the bolt again, she walked over to the window to check, but the road was still clear of cars. The rain was ending.

She returned to bed. Alex hopped back up and snuggled against her. Hugging him to her, she lay back down on the bed and allowed the hypnotic sound of the water crashing against the rocks on the shore to lull her back to sleep.

Her clock read 9:30 A.M.

At first Quinn didn't believe it. She never slept that late, even on vacation.

Her eyes took in every aspect of the room. How different it looked in daylight! The wallpaper had bright blue and violet flowers on it, the same color blue as the Queen Anne chair and in the pattern of the curtains that were now hanging limply by the window.

Outside, as far as she could see was calm blue sea. There was nothing remaining of the stormy anger from last night. Close up, she could see parts of the sand and rocky beach. There were some steps leading to the water. Two white sails, like clouds, crossed the horizon. Save for that sign of civilization, it would be easy to think she was alone in the world.

From her other window she saw the road, surrounded by short trees, some pines and flat bogs. In the distance, she could see some buildings. She leaned out the window and managed to see part of the driveway. Her father's Mercedes was in the driveway, and so was Ben's sports car, and a Japanese car, probably for Beverly.

Quinn let her sense of smell guide her to the kitchen. She had expected to see others at the breakfast table, and was disappointed to find the room empty, the table cluttered with remains of the morning meal.

A half pot of coffee brewed in the warmer. Searching the cabinets, she took a moment to find a mug that was neither stained nor chipped. Beverly certainly wasn't the housekeeper her mother was. Mom would never have even left the room with dishes on the table.

Quinn poured a cup of the dark brew and tasted it. Not bad; not great, either. Scooping up the bacon crumbs still on the platter, Quinn nibbled them and then glanced around the room. Should she find Beverly or should she make her own breakfast? Was she still a guest, even if she was living here? She opened the fridge. Not much. Well, the English muffin would have to do, she thought, taking the last one and putting it into the toaster.

The muffin popped just as hands touched her shoulders.

"Hello, princess."

Breathless, she turned. "Hello, Daddy. You scared me!"

"Sorry." David Philips reached out to the toaster to retrieve her English muffin. "You sleep okay last night?"

Quinn drained the last of the juice from the glass. "Yeah, fine," she lied.

"You've certainly slept late enough. I thought you usually got up early."

"Usually." She buttered the muffin and took it over to the table where her coffee cup sat.

"You're not glad to see me?"

"Sure I am." Her back was to him. She took a bite of the toasted muffin.

"But you haven't hugged me."

"I don't hug strange men."

"Quinn!" There was hurt in his voice. He pulled out a chair, the legs scraping against the linoleum, and sat down. "I guess I deserved that. But, honey, I'm going to make it up to you. You'll see—this summer together will be great."

"Sure."

"I've even taken off the summer from teaching at the university. I'll have to do some work on my book, but I'll also spend time with you. We can sail and fish."

"I don't fish. I never did."

"Sure you did, Quinn."

"When I was six, you dragged me out on that boat because you wanted me to like fishing. You wanted me to be a boy. All I remember is hating those worms, feeling hot and hating the way those poor fish were squirming, dying in the sun. You're wrong, Daddy. I never liked fishing, but then you wouldn't know. You were never around to ask me what I liked."

"Quinn..." He reached his hand out to cover hers.

There was a moment of silence.

"Since when did you start drinking coffee?"

"Last year." It wasn't a lie. Mom had given her a cup of coffee the year before.

"Really." Her father's voice was strained. "My little girl is growing up."

"I'm not a little girl anymore."

"Oh, Quinn, sweetheart, you'll always be my little girl."

She took a huge gulp of the coffee, trying to maintain some sense of control.

"I'm glad you've come, Quinn."

"I didn't have much choice, did I? I mean, Mom was going on her honeymoon with Paul. She wouldn't let me stay with any of my friends. She—"

"How is your mother?"

"Fine."

"She happy?"

"I guess."

"You like Paul?"

"Sure. He's nice."

"Nicer than me, you mean?" He reached out and took the second half of her English muffin. The only sound at that moment was the crunching of the bread. Her own muffin on the plate was unfinished.

Quinn shrugged. "He's nice. We get along. He talks to me."

"We'll talk. This summer. I promise, princess. You'll have to excuse Beverly—the way the house is, I mean. Not enough supplies. She's been busy on some political project."

"Is that what you were doing last night?"

He gave her a quizzical look.

"I mean, the reason you couldn't pick me up from Boston. Mom had told me you would. Then when they paged me and told me to take the bus . . ."

"You took the bus from Boston at night? Ben was supposed to pick you up from the airport."

"No, the message said he would pick me up from Falmouth. Only I made a mistake and got off the bus in Woods Hole and—"

"Oh, baby, Quinn, baby. Sweetie, I'm so sorry. I'll have to talk to Ben about it. You shouldn't have had to take the bus."

"It's okay." She shrugged him off. "I didn't mind."

"But I do. What happened after you left the bus? Was he there?"

Quinn saw no reason to get off on the wrong foot with her new stepbrother or tell her father that Ben had come roaring down the road, nearly killing her. She certainly wasn't going to say that he dropped her off at the house and left her alone. "He was there and everything worked out fine."

"Good, good. But, he should have been at the airport!"

Quinn pressed her lips together. Her father should have been at the airport, not Ben, but why argue with him about that?

"The main thing is that you're here and you're fine. Come on. I'll take you to meet your new mother."

"Stepmother."

"Right. Stepmother."

He guided her out of the kitchen and along the long downstairs hall filled with paintings of Harris ancestors.

"Mom told you that Alex was coming with me, didn't she?" she asked.

"Who?"

"Alexander the Great. My cat. You remember. He's the one who was always chewing your slippers. Ben says his mother doesn't like cats."

"The cat. Oh, yes, yes. I recall. You say you brought him?"

"I told Mom I was going to. She said she'd tell you."

"She probably did, and I forgot to tell Beverly." He smiled ruefully.

"But Dad, he's here with me."

"Where?"

"Upstairs. In my room. You were supposed to buy him litter and cat food."

"Was I? Well, we can go into town and get some later."

"But what about Beverly?"

David Philips squeezed his daughter's arm affectionately. "I'll work it out. Don't worry. As long as you keep Alex quiet, things will be okay."

"You mean you're not going to tell her? Dad, you're making a mistake. Ben'll tell her if you don't."

"Well, don't worry, princess. It'll be okay. He's here with you and you'll take care of him. There won't be any problems—as long as you keep him quiet."

"I promise." She thought of how Alex had been pawing at the door last night, and again this morning. She would have to find a scratching post for him when she went into town.

Her father opened the door to Beverly's studio, which faced the sea. The view here was the same as Quinn's: a rocky beach and the expansive blue ocean. All the windows were open, and a brisk breeze bounced off the bare walls and floors.

"Bev?" David Philips called out. "Beverly? Where are you?" He touched his daughter's hand. "You wait here, Quinn. She could be in the back, and she doesn't like to be disturbed when she's working. I'll get her."

Quinn nodded. She watched as her father walked through the open French doors and around the side. Then she turned her attention to the half-complete sculpture before her. The figure looked like a man—but no ordinary man. His head was twice as large as his body, and his upper limbs were exaggerated in such a way that he seemed grotesque. Quinn wondered if Bev had done that on purpose, or if she really didn't know how to sculpt.

Another sculpture, one made of clay that still seemed to be wet, reminded Quinn of an African mask she had seen in a textbook. The eyes especially held her attention, and she reached out to touch the impassive face.

"Get away from there!" someone screamed.

Startled, Quinn drew back to see a young woman not much older than herself. Her ash-blond hair framed a heart-shaped face. Her face, which a moment ago had been distorted in rage, now calmed as if the mask itself had slipped over it.

"I'm sorry, honey. It's just that I worry about the clay being dry."

"I wasn't going to hurt anything."

"I know. I know." Her voice now was sweet and melodic, like a practiced singer's.

David Philips stepped up behind. His large hand covered the slender woman's shoulder. "Beverly, darling, meet my daughter, Quinn."

# Chapter Four

The whole area once belonged to my grandfather and the family before." Beverly smiled at Quinn across a tuna salad lunch on the patio. "The Harrises came over with Roger Williams and settled the area. For as far as you could see—" her slender arm gestured toward the ocean and the land "—it belonged to us." She shrugged. "Now, of course, progress and the high cost of living made our family sell off much of the forest land. You can see one of the condo developments over there." She pointed to the northwest. Then she scooped more tuna onto Quinn's plate.

Quinn eyed the fish and salad combination. Mom made her tuna plain with just mayonnaise and diced carrots. Beverly had put everything under the sun into this, or so it seemed. She watched her father eating his salad with pleasure and wondered if he didn't miss her mother's cooking.

She nibbled a bite more and took a cracker. This was worse than the tuna they had at school. If this kept up, she wouldn't have to worry about going on that diet when she got home.

Lost in thought, staring out at the crashing waves and the gulls beyond, Quinn barely realized that Beverly was speaking to her.

"I hope we'll be a real family this summer—Dave, you, Ben and me."

"Oh. Yeah." Quinn had been thinking about the boy she had met the other night and wanted to ask about him, but her instincts told her not to. Ben hadn't liked him, and she didn't want to get Beverly upset with her so early in her stay.

There was something about Beverly that Quinn couldn't quite pinpoint. On the surface, she seemed so nice, yet there was that inner tightness Quinn felt whenever Beverly smiled at her. "This house isn't haunted, is it?" she asked abruptly.

"Why would you ask that, Quinn?" Again, that strange smile.

Quinn thought about the night before, about the way the shadows had played on the walls. She was sure someone had been in the room with her. Handles didn't turn by themselves.

"Just asked. It seems like it would be."

"To tell you the truth, I haven't met any of them, but my mother, who lived here before me, and her mother both swore they met my great-great-grandfather, who had drowned at sea, and his father, who had been killed by the Indians."

"Really?" Quinn felt the hair on the back of her neck rise. "I did think I heard something last night."

Beverly patted her hand. "I doubt it was the ghosts. It could have been the wind whistling through some of the loose boards. This is an old house, you know. And being so isolated on the tip of land, we're more exposed to the elements.''

"Yeah, maybe that was it."

Her father gave a low groan.

"Something wrong, darling?" Beverly turned to Quinn's father.

He shook his head. "No, just my darned ulcer acting up." His face was contorted with pain.

"I didn't know you had an ulcer, Dad."

David Philips shrugged. "With all the stress this past year, the divorce and all... But things are bound to improve in this perfect place. I can look out at the sea, think, write, and I have Beverly." He raised his hand to her in a loving gesture, and smiling at him, she took it.

Quinn felt the anger rising in her. How could her father show love to another woman in front of her? Didn't he care about her feelings? Didn't he think she owed some loyalty to her mother?

It was funny, though, seeing Mom and Paul look into each other's eyes hadn't bothered her in the same way. Maybe it was because she knew that Paul really loved her mother—and somehow in the few hours since she had met Beverly, she didn't believe this woman loved her father. She had heard about sirens who lured ships away to crash on the rocks. Bev was a siren. She had lured her father away.

"You finished eating, Quinn?"

"Yeah, Dad." She put down her plate, then, remembering her manners, picked it up again to take it into the kitchen.

"That's okay, Quinn." Beverly gave her a cheerleader smile. "I'll take care of everything. You're our guest."

"Okay. If you're sure."

"Positive."

Somehow, Quinn didn't feel as positive, but she did as Beverly asked and replaced the plate on the wrought-iron table. Then she glanced down toward the beach steps. Some of them were broken. If she were careful . . .

"You can walk there later, Quinn. Right now, I need to talk to you in my study," her dad interrupted her thoughts.

"About Mom?"

"No, about us—and your future."

"Okay, but I gotta go take care of Alex first. I want to make sure he's okay."

"My study is the second door down from the right. Knock hard. If I'm working I don't always hear."

The oak door, which her father had indicated, was closed.

With her free hand, Quinn pounded. "Dad! Dad!"

There was no answer. Alex squirmed in her arms, but she held him tight. She didn't want him running around the house now.

She knocked again. "Dad! It's me!" Even if he was working, she had certainly shouted loud enough. Maybe he's not in there, she thought, as she turned the knob.

The door swung open, creaking on its unoiled hinges.

"Dad!" Quinn dropped Alexander and rushed forward to the desk where her father was slumped over some papers. "Dad!"

"Beverly! Ben! Come quick. Dad's unconscious."

She picked up the phone. "Help me!" She cried out to the operator who answered. "My father, he's unconscious. He's…yes, this is the Harris house. I don't know where exactly. Woods Hole. I…yes, thank you." She shouted into the hall. "Beverly! Beverly! Come quick! Dad's hurt!"

Rushing back to her father's side, Quinn tried to remember what she had learned in her first-aid class. All she could think of was to keep him warm, so she threw his jacket over him.

It was only when she heard the siren coming up the road that she spotted Beverly in the garden. Where had she been? Hadn't she heard her call? Quinn watched as Beverly met the paramedics and followed them into the house.

Quinn ran to her stepmother as they entered the room.

"What's wrong? What happened to David?" Beverly asked.

The two attendants put Quinn's father onto a stretcher and carried him to the ambulance.

There, with the application of oxygen, her father regained consciousness.

"What happened, baby?" he asked.

"That's what I'd like to know. You told me to come down to see you and when you didn't answer my knock, I went in and found you slumped over the desk."

"Beverly must have called the paramedics, then."

"Right," Quinn answered. She didn't want her father to know that Beverly hadn't been around until the last moment.

"Where is she?"

"Who? Oh, Beverly? She's following us in her car. I wanted to ride with you, and the men said it was okay."

"I'm glad." He squeezed her hand, but his grasp was weaker than usual. "I'm glad you're here with me this summer, Quinn. We've got a lot of talking to do. I have plans for you."

She laid his hand down by his side. "Why don't you rest now? We can talk about your plans later."

He smiled before closing his eyes.

Later Quinn watched as the nurse took her father's blood pressure, pulse and respiration.

"How are you feeling, Daddy?"

"Fine, sweetheart. Where's Beverly?"

"She's coming. I told you. She was following us and probably stopped to get Ben or something."

About twenty minutes later, the doctor came in, followed by the nurse and Beverly.

"Well, Mr. Philips, you're going to be just fine," the doctor said heartily.

"Why did my father pass out like that? He can't be fine if he passes out."

"Young lady, your father had a mild form of food poisoning combined with an allergic reaction to something. Not quite sure what it was, but the Benedryl injection we gave him seems to have taken care of it." He turned to Quinn's father. "I would watch what I eat from now on, Mr. Philips. You're lucky that your daughter found you in time and had the presence of mind to call the paramedics."

Quinn flushed.

"I'll leave a prescription for you at the front desk, Mr. Philips, in case this thing happens again. But mind, you have to take it as soon as you start to feel woozy."

"I'll watch him," Beverly said. She turned to her husband. "You all set then, darling?"

He nodded.

Beverly helped him off the table and kissed him. "I can't tell you how relieved I am that you're all right. But what I don't understand is why you didn't call me, Quinn?"

"I did," Quinn protested. "Several times."

"Really?" Beverly's voice was mockingly skeptical.

"Oh, I forgot. You had a call today," Ben told Quinn over dinner a few nights later.

"Really? Who?"

"Some guy."

"Who?"

"Don't know. He hung up when I answered the phone. Probably Logan James. Would be just like him to call and hang up."

Quinn flushed. "Did he leave a number?"

"Nope. Told you. He didn't say anything. I'm only guessing that it's James."

"Oh." She wondered if she should phone him.

Ben seemed to read her mind. "The Jameses don't have a phone at home, so I wouldn't bother trying to find a number for them. If he wants to call you, he will."

"Yeah. Sure." Quinn gulped down the rest of her milk, trying to act as if boys called her every day. "Excuse me." She moved away from the table.

"Where are you going, honey?" her father asked.

"Upstairs. I want to...check on Alex."

She heard Beverly mutter something about the cat and winced. Poor Alex.

"After you check on Alex, we need to talk, Quinn."

"Aren't you tired, Dad? Don't you want to rest? I mean we have the whole summer to talk."

There was a moment of silence before he nodded. "Okay, but don't forget."

"I won't," she promised. Her mind kept repeating one thought. Logan had said he would call and he had.

It was only as she reached the top did she recall that he said she should call him if she wanted to talk. That meant he must have a phone. Why had Ben lied to her?

# Chapter Five

Quinn could hear the murmur of voices below and wondered if Dad and Beverly were talking about her.

Alex hopped over to her purse and began to dig inside with his paws.

"I said no more for you, Alex!" Quinn zipped up the compartment where the candy was. That cat was too smart for his own good. "One day that curiosity of yours is going to get you into trouble." She scooped him up in her arms just as the sound of a car's ignition startled them both. Ever anxious to find out what was happening, Alex leaped over to the windowsill.

Quinn followed him. Ben's car had disappeared. She wondered where he was going. On a date? She turned her attention toward the shore and the waves pounding the surf. From this view, it seemed that the house was the only one in the world and that they were far more isolated than they really were.

"See you later," she told the cat, and slipped out her bedroom room, closing the door behind her. She hurried downstairs to the den.

"Hi!"

"Oh, hello, princess." David Philips came over and gave his daughter a big hug. "I'm glad you decided to join us, after all."

Quinn felt Beverly staring at her. Yes, she was sure they had been talking about her. There was tension in the air. "Anything doing tonight? I mean, I don't see a TV."

"We don't believe in television here," Beverly responded coldly.

"No television?"

"Darling, we do have a television, but it's upstairs in our room. The fact is we seldom watch it except for the news. There are many other things to do here," her father answered. "Exploring the beach, picking cranberries, the movies. We even have a couple of museums in town and there're several cute little shops. I'm sure you'll want to bring something home for your mother."

"Oh, right."

Beverly leaned over and kissed him. "Sweetheart, why don't you have your talk with your daughter now. I'll go finish my sculpture and then we can have hot buttered rums by the fire."

"Good idea, darling." His eyes were soft with love as he watched her leave the room.

Quinn couldn't help feeling jealous anger rising in her. He didn't appreciate that it was she who had found him! Beverly couldn't have cared less! No, that wasn't true. Still he was making himself into a fool with his new wife. When had he ever kissed and hugged Mom like that? Certainly not in Quinn's memory.

"Earth to Quinn!" Her father was waving his hand in front of her face.

"Oh, sorry. Guess I was thinking."

"Yes, I guess you were. Come sit down over here, princess." He motioned toward the leather sofa.

"You sure you feel okay?" she asked.

"Never felt better. I'm not really sure what happened last week, but I guess I've developed some sort of allergy I wasn't aware of. Those things can happen."

"I guess." She folded her arms and stared into the fire. There were several moments of silence as her father puffed away on his pipe.

"So tell me. How's school?"

"Fine since I'm not there now."

"You're doing well?"

Quinn shrugged. "Got an A in history."

"Anything else?"

"B in biology, B in home ec, C in French, C in math, C− in gym, D+ in music."

"You didn't like music, I take it."

"Music's fine. Why do you want to know? You never asked me about my grades when you lived with us. You always had Mom sign my report card."

"Well, things have changed. I've been investigating schools. There's an excellent girls' academy in Hyannisport."

Quinn gazed around the room with its high wooden rafters and row upon row of bookcases, and the huge picture windows that looked out to sea. Water for as far as one could look. Easy to drown her thoughts there.

"What do you say, Quinn?"

"About what?"

"About staying out here for your senior year?"

She sat upright. "I can't leave Mom now."

"She has Paul. Don't you think she wants to be alone for a bit with him?"

"Well, don't you want to be alone with Beverly?"

"Quinn, that's not the issue. The issue is that I have money and I want you to have the very best education. After your senior year here, I'll send you to Radcliffe."

"I don't want to go to Radcliffe. I want to stay in Illinois. I want to finish high school there and go to the University of Illinois with Cathy and Jen."

"You'll make other friends out here."

"I've been best friends with Cathy and Jen since we were in fourth grade together on the north side."

"Oh, yes. Clinton Grade School. Darling, this will be much better for your future."

Surely her mother couldn't have agreed! "Did you ask Mommy?" She flushed. "I mean, Mom."

"No, princess. I haven't asked your mother yet. I wanted to talk to you first. Quinn, I want you to have the very best."

"The very best for me would have been if you had stayed with Mom and me." She saw the stricken look on his face and felt guilty. What was done was done and the past couldn't be repeated. "I'll wait and hear what Mom has to say about school." She stood and grabbed her sweater.

"Where are you going, Quinn?"

She sighed. "On the beach. I want to take a walk."

"Think about what I've been saying, princess. We'll talk about it again, but I have to tell the school soon."

"Dad, I don't want to leave Evanston. I like where I am. I want to be a vet and take care of animals like Alex."

"I'm sure there's a good veterinary program out here." Her father paused and put down his pipe. "Okay, we'll leave it for now. Be careful on the beach. It'll be getting dark soon. I don't want you out there at night."

"Sure."

Without looking back, Quinn opened the French doors and started down the path to the beach. A wind was coming in from the east. Quinn shivered as she zipped up her sweater. Carefully she made her way down the rocky path to the sandy beach where the tide was just now receding. She walked along the wet sand, feeling it squishing under the soles of her tennis shoes. She should have worn beach clogs, but no matter. Her shoes were old, anyway.

Standing by the water, she looked out toward the deepening blue horizon. It felt as if she was standing on the edge of the world, as

if all she had to do was take one step and all
her cares would disappear. Dad didn't really
care about her or her feelings. She wiped her
eyes on her sweater sleeve. All he wanted was
what looked best.

"Well, he should have thought about that
before he left us," she said out loud.

"What did you say?" the voice behind her
asked.

Quickly Quinn spun about. His eyes were
the color of the sea even in the dimming light.

"What did you say?" Logan repeated.

"I . . . I was just talking to myself."

"Did your stepbrother give you my message?"

"He told me some boy called for me, but he
didn't tell me who."

"I guess that was to be expected. Well, I'm
glad I saw you tonight, anyway. I wanted to see
how you had settled in."

"Oh. I'm fine."

"Heard there was some excitement at the
house last week. Your father okay now?"

Quinn nodded. "How'd you know about
that?"

His grin was like a jack-o-lantern lit up. "Can't live in a small town like Woods Hole and not hear these things. Besides, I was at the coffee shop when Beverly came in to find Ben. He is all right now, isn't he?"

Quinn nodded again.

"Better be careful. That's the second time in less than two months that he's been in the emergency room. Surprised the doctor didn't say something."

"Did he have food poisoning then, too? Or an allergy?"

"Don't know. You'll have to ask him. I think he blacked out from a headache."

"Dad never had headaches before."

"Stress, I guess."

"Yeah," Quinn responded, looking up toward the house. She noticed several lights were on, including the one in her father's study. "I guess." She forced herself to smile at him. "I would have called you back, if I had known—"

"Doesn't matter." Logan bent and picked up a piece of driftwood. "I was coming down here, anyway." He pointed to the pile of wood in the corner. "Driftwood. The best seems to come in here. I collect it for my mother's shop. Mom owns a gift shop in town. She makes things out of the driftwood and shells. Popular with the tourists."

"Oh. Does Beverly sell her sculptures there?"

He laughed. "No way. She'd never lower herself to sell her things in our shop. In case you haven't guessed, Quinn, our two families aren't exactly on the best of terms."

"Why not?"

Before he could answer, Quinn heard her name being called. Looking up, she could see her father standing on the very edge of the rocky precipice calling her name.

"Guess I'd better go back now. It's getting dark. Dad didn't want me out here too late." She paused a moment, wanting to say something more and yet not finding anything to say.

"Quinn?"

"Yes?"

"You free tomorrow night?"

"I guess so."

"Good. How about the movies?"

"You mean a date?"

"Why not?"

"I…" She glanced up toward her father and waved in his direction. "Yeah, sure."

"Okay, I'll see you then. Be waiting outside at seven-thirty. I'd rather not go in and hassle with Beverly, if you don't mind."

"I can understand that," she said. "I'll be waiting."

## Chapter Six

"Who is it?"

"Me, princess."

Quinn sighed and went to open the door for her father. She wondered if he was going to insist on talking about the school issue again. She had barely seen him all day. He had been cloistered in his study working on his research material for a new book. For that matter she hadn't seen much of Beverly or Ben, either. But that was all right with her.

"Hello, Daddy."

"Going out?" He looked at the clothes on her bed. "Looks like you're having trouble deciding what to wear."

Quinn glanced at the items on her bed and then at her father. Ben hadn't been too fond of Logan. Maybe her father wasn't either. She hoped he wasn't going to forbid her from going on the date—not now.

Quinn shook her head. "I was just sorting through my clothes. Mom packed for me and I didn't know what I had." Well, that really wasn't a lie. Mother had done most of the packing. Quinn held her breath, hoping her father would accept what she said.

"What do you want to do tonight?"

"Tonight?" Her voice was like an untuned piano. "Thought I'd take a walk and do some sketching."

He seemed to believe her.

"Dinner ready?"

"Shortly. But I wanted to talk to you about tonight, honey. Bev and I have another meeting. She just reminded me about it. Do you mind staying alone for a few hours?"

"No, I don't mind."

"Good. We'll have dinner within a half hour." He leaned over to kiss her. But the kiss didn't feel like her father's old kisses. This man was a stranger. "Quinn, I'm glad you're here."

"Yeah, me too." She hoped he didn't feel her nervousness.

"I hope you're thinking about that school. We'll talk about it again tomorrow."

"Okay."

At 7:25 P.M., Quinn took one last look in the mirror. Had she put the makeup on correctly? Her palms were sweaty. Would Logan notice? Would he know that this was her very first date?

The sound of a car coming up the road brought her back to her senses, and grabbing her purse and a sweater, she started down the steps, only to return for her drawing pad. At least if her father saw her later, she could tell him she had been sketching. Besides, Logan might want to see her pictures.

She was out of the house in a moment and waiting at the entrance when Logan pulled up.

Only as she got into the truck did she see the curtains moving at the top of the house. Ben was watching her! Would he tell her dad?

But within moments of leaving the house, she had forgotten about Ben and Beverly Harris.

They saw a foreign movie, *Camilia*. It made Quinn wish she had taken Spanish rather than French, but the subtitles explained almost everything, and Logan whispered certain phrases to her that hadn't come up in translation. Later they walked through the town, pausing a moment in front of a tourist shop. Logan explained that this was where his mother sold her driftwood and shell statues. Quinn picked up a small carpeted stand. It would make a good scratching post for Alex.

"Come on," Logan said, taking her by the hand to lead her through the store to a petite woman standing near the paintings. He introduced his mother, Madeline James, to Quinn. He took Quinn's sketchbook from her. "Mom, I want you to see her drawings."

"Logan!" Quinn felt the lobster-red flush creeping up her cheeks.

"These are good, especially the cat!" Mrs. James said admiringly. "You ought to have professional training."

"That's Alexander the Great. He's with me at the Harris house this summer."

"The Harris house? Oh, you're David's daughter."

Quinn smiled.

"How do you like your new stepmother?" Madeline James asked as Quinn touched the smoothness of a shell doll.

"Mother!" Logan's voice cut in. "That's not a fair question. Quinn hasn't been here long."

"Maybe not," Madeline James said, "but don't let her upset you, honey. Bev has a way of alienating people."

"Why don't we go have some ice cream?" Logan suggested quickly. "Mom's in a strange mood right now."

Quinn nodded, though she really wanted to continue the conversation with Mrs. James. She wanted to know everything about her stepmother.

With a sigh, she had to admit to herself that until Mom's wedding to Paul she had kind of hoped that her folks would get back together. Now, of course, it was too late.

Logan put his arm around her shoulders as he led her along the street past the Marine Biology Lab, which looked more like an old stone tavern from Colonial times. It even had the wooden ship protruding from the second floor ledge. "That used to be a supply store," he told her, guiding her along the cobbled street. "They sold spermaceti candles and other things to the whalers."

Quinn turned back to study the building again. What secrets could be learned if those stones could talk? Or if the Harris house could talk? Suddenly she shivered. The talking house reminded her of her dream and besides, she didn't like thinking of the house on the precipice, isolated as it seemed from other dwellings.

Quinn and Logan found seats in the outdoor café overlooking the harbor. In the cool and dark of the night, she could imagine the large sails, white in the moonlight, belonging to the huge clipper ships of old.

"Penny for your thoughts?"

"I don't know they're even worth that."

Logan took her hand. "Try me."

"I was only thinking about Dad and Mom and—"

"And Beverly?"

"Yeah, and Beverly. Why is it you don't get along with the Harrises?"

He shrugged. "I'd say it was the other way around. They don't get along with me."

"But why?"

Logan stood and, taking out money for their ice cream, put it on the table under the rose vase. "Come on, I'd better get you back."

"You haven't answered my question."

"Let's go." He took her hand and led her back to the car. He didn't speak again until they were nearly at the door to the house.

"Can I ask you out again?"

"Can you?" She had never in a million, zillion years thought that this would happen this summer at Dad's. "Uh, sure."

"Good. I'll be in touch. Give my regards to your cat."

Before Quinn could answer he leaned over to kiss her gently.

Then, like a ghost, he was gone.

Quinn stared after the disappearing truck. After a few moments, she realized that she was getting chilled and should go in.

Dad's car wasn't in the driveway, so she didn't have to worry about him, but she noticed Ben's Porsche. She hurried upstairs to her room where she could hear Alex crying at the door and pawing to be let out.

"Hello, baby. Hello, boy." Hugging him, she heard the contented purr as she stroked him. He licked her face and told her in no uncertain terms that he was hungry.

"But I just filled up your bowl." Quinn looked down, amazed to see that the cat food had disappeared.

"Okay, boy." She poured more cat food into the container and watched as he greedily ate it.

She had only put the container down when a knock at her door startled her.

"Open up," Ben demanded.

"The door is open."

Alex perked his ears and stopped eating. His back raised and he hissed as Ben stepped into the room.

"You'd better keep control of your animal. I won't be responsible if anything happens to him."

Glaring at her stepbrother, Quinn picked up the cat. "Hush, Alex." She stroked his ears, hoping he would calm down, and kept a tight hold on him.

"Where did you go tonight?"

"Out."

"With Logan James?"

Quinn shrugged. "He drove me, yes."

"I don't think you should see him."

"I don't think you have any right to tell me who I can and cannot see. You aren't my father."

"No, but your father feels the same way about the Jameses as Beverly and I do."

"Oh? Why?"

"Does it matter? I forbid you to see that fellow anymore."

"I don't take orders from you."

"Then I'll have to tell your father about your evening plans. I'm sure he didn't know."

"He knew I was going out."

"Well, then we'll see what Beverly has to say about the matter."

She opened her door, still holding on to the fighting cat. "Yes, I guess we will, but meanwhile I'm tired and Alex doesn't like you in our room."

Ben took the hint.

# Chapter Seven

Quinn sat down next to her father and poured herself a generous glass of orange juice. "Hi, Dad. How was your meeting last night?"

David Philips lowered the paper slightly. He smiled at her. "Fine. You have a good time sketching?"

"Uh, yeah."

Bev put a plate of bacon and eggs on the table. Quinn took a piece of toast and began to butter it.

"Where'd you go?" he asked.

She was aware that Beverly was still standing by the table.

"Oh, just around."

"Dave..."

Her father turned toward his wife. He dropped the paper. "I'll handle this, Bev. Finish what you're doing."

Trying to act nonchalant, Quinn took a bite of her toast.

"Where did you go, Quinn?"

"To town. A friend gave me a lift."

"A friend?" David put his coffee cup down on the table. "What friend? You haven't been on the Cape long enough to make friends with anyone."

"That's not true. I met him the first day. He helped me get out to the house here when Ben didn't meet me."

"What do you mean, Ben didn't meet you? I thought you told me he picked you up."

"I told you, Dad. He only met me later. The message told me to get off at Falmouth and—"

"Why Falmouth? That's several miles farther down the road." His paper had fallen on the floor now. "Bev, what do you know about this?"

Quinn's stepmother shrugged. "Dave, honey, Ben told me he would take care of everything. We'll have to ask him."

"May I be excused, please?" Quinn asked.

"Not so fast, Quinn. We still have to discuss this date last night."

"It wasn't a real date. I mean, I—"

"Why didn't your friend come up to meet me? The proper thing would have been to say hello to your parents."

"You weren't home."

"Are you saying that he came by without phoning? Quinn, what is this fellow's name?"

"Logan."

"Logan what?"

"It can only be Logan James," Beverly said, coming back over to the table with another batch of bacon. Pouring coffee, she sat down. "He's part of the family I told you about."

"If I had known that, Quinn, I would have forbidden you from the start."

"Dad, there's nothing wrong with Logan James. He's very nice."

# First
# Class
# Romance

## Delivered to your door by
## First Love from Silhouette®

# Find romance at your door with 4 FREE First Love from Silhouette novels!

Sent right to your home...books that you will treasure for their unusual plots, their unconventional love stories... unpredictable characters to surprise and delight you... stories written just for you, about you and your friends.

You can receive these stories each month to read at home. All you have to do is fill out and mail back the attached postage-paid order card, and you'll get 4 new First Love from Silhouette novels absolutely FREE! It's a $7.80 value...plus we'll send you a FREE Folding Umbrella and a Mystery Gift. And there's another bonus: our monthly First Love from Silhouette Newsletter, free with your subscription.

After you receive your free books, you'll have the chance to preview 4 more First Love from Silhouette novels for 15 days. If you decide to keep them, you'll pay just $7.80— with no extra charge for home delivery and at no risk! You'll also have the option of cancelling at any time. Just drop us a note. Your first 4 books, Folding Umbrella and Mystery Gift are yours to keep in any case.

*First Love from Silhouette* ®

**A FREE**
*Folding
Umbrella and
Mystery Gift
await you, too!*

CLIP AND MAIL THIS POSTPAID CARD TODAY!

# Mail this card today for
## 4 FREE BOOKS
### (a $7.80 value)
### and a Folding Umbrella and Mystery Gift FREE!

*First Love from Silhouette* ®

**Silhouette Books, 120 Brighton Rd., P.O. Box 5084, Clifton, NJ 07015-9956**

☐ YES! Please send me my four First Love from Silhouette novels FREE, along with my FREE Folding Umbrella and Mystery Gift, as explained in this insert. I understand that I am under no obligation to purchase any books.

NAME _____

(please print)

ADDRESS _____

CITY _____ STATE _____ ZIP _____

Terms and prices subject to change.
Your enrollment is subject to acceptance by Silhouette Books.

First Love from Silhouette is a registered trademark.

CMF066

"That's not the point, Quinn. The point is that the boy isn't suitable for you."

"But he is. We have a lot in common. We both like animals and . . . and he's promised to show me around."

"Ben can show you around."

"Dad, you're not being fair. Logan's a nice guy. I like him, and I plan to see him again while I'm here. If you don't want me to, send me back to Evanston. I'll stay with Cathy or Jen." She poured orange juice and gulped it down.

"Quinn, dear," Beverly said. "Let's be reasonable. I understand how you feel, but you don't know the James family the way I do. Believe me, you'd be wise to avoid them. They're bad news. Logan was involved in drugs for a while. In fact, there was some suspicion that he might be a dealer."

Quinn's mouth fell open. She had never thought of someone like Logan doing anything like that. The drug users and pushers she had seen at school were all slick, well-dressed guys—more like Ben than like Logan. "Was he arrested? Did he spend time in jail?"

Bev shook her head. "Unfortunately as soon as word leaked out that there was an investigation, the drug traffic stopped momentarily. So no one could prove that Logan was the leader."

"Then how do you know he was?"

"He goes away sometimes, and his return has always coincided with a heavier use in the town. Sometimes even with several deaths."

"But that's all circumstantial." She wanted to defend Logan, and yet she didn't really know enough about him.

"Well, in any case, we don't want you to see him," her father interjected.

"As your father said before, Ben can take you around any place you want to go," Beverly added.

"Don't go making promises for me, Mother, dear." Ben came into the kitchen. His hair, still wet from the shower, was slicked back like that of a punk rocker. A cashmere sweater was casually tied about his broad shoulders.

"Ben, your stepsister wants to see some of the Cape. Be a darling and take her with you today."

His look told Quinn all she needed to know. It was exactly as she'd told Paul back in Chicago. Ben thought of her as a drag. Well, she didn't care, she didn't want to go with him, either.

"Quinn, dear—" Beverly pushed the glass of milk forward as Quinn reached for the coffee "—we do have plans to keep you busy this summer. You'll see. But for now it would be wise to stay away from the James family."

"But, Dad, Logan's a nice guy. I'm sure he's not into drugs."

"You can never be sure these days. I agree with Bev. You're to stay away from that boy and his family. I forbid you to have any contact with them while you're here."

Quinn willed herself to remain calm. But it was hard not to see the smug look on Ben's face. Of course, he had told them about her date. It wasn't fair! Her first boyfriend and Dad playing the heavy-handed father. There was no way Logan could be involved in drugs. She threw down her napkin and pushed away from the table.

"Where are you going now, darling?" her father asked.

"My room, I guess."

"We're not finished."

"I thought we were. You told me not to see Logan."

"Quinn, I want your agreement on this."

"Why?"

"Because I said so, young woman. You are to give me your solemn promise that you will not see this boy."

"And what if I see him by accident? What if I'm in town and—"

"You can be polite, of course. I certainly wouldn't want my daughter to be rude to anyone."

"You know he helped me—when no one else would." Her voice choked. "Fat lot you cared about me. You weren't even around."

"Quinn!" He paused. "I told you, I'll look into the matter. Meanwhile, I want a promise from you that you'll not see this Logan James."

Silence.

"Well?"

"Yeah, okay." Behind her back, Quinn crossed her fingers. "May I leave now?"

Her father nodded.

Quinn turned and fled up the stairs.

# Chapter Eight

Ben honked the horn and Quinn ran down the steps. Well, at least she was getting out of the house and into town.

She glanced toward her father's study. Why did he invite her out here this summer if he was going to be working on his book all the time? You'd think after the accident the other day that he'd want to take it easy a bit more. But if anything, he had thrown himself more into the work than she remembered him doing at home.

She reached the door. "Can I drive?"

"Can you what?" Ben's voice rose an octave. "Drive my Porsche? You've got to be crazy!"

"I'm not crazy. I have my student permit."

"Listen, do you want to go to town or not?"

Quinn nodded.

"Then hop in." Ben pushed the car door open for her.

Silently she slid into the seat next to him. She hadn't been in this car since the day she'd arrived, when he had met her and Logan on the road. She had barely closed the door before he pressed the accelerator. The car roared onto the road, taking off like a rocket.

"Hey! You want to kill me or something?" Quinn asked, buckling her seat belt.

Ben's response was to press the gas pedal to the floor. This time, Quinn had to hang on to the seat to keep from being thrown.

They arrived in town in less than twenty minutes—nearly half the time it had taken with Logan the night before.

Quinn had to sit a moment after he had parked the car by the harbor before she was able to get out. "Why were you driving so fast?"

"I like going fast. Listen, I've got some business to do in town. Can you take care of yourself for a while?"

"Sure."

"Meet you at the café over there at—" he glanced at his watch "—four o'clock."

Quinn nodded. That was the same place she and Logan had had their ice cream the night before. "Okay."

She watched him run down the street toward the marine museum and enter through a side door. What did he have to do in town that was so important?

Well, it didn't matter. Quinn was just as happy to be alone and have a moment to speak to Mrs. James. Would Logan be at the store? He'd told her he often helped out.

In a way, she wanted to see him but in another way, she hoped he wasn't there. She had the feeling that Mrs. James would be able to tell her something about Beverly that she needed to know. She walked slowly to the gift store and opened the old, painted door.

An elderly man stood behind the counter.

"May I help you, miss?"

"Uh, no. I was just waiting for someone."

"May I ask who?"

"Mrs. James."

"She doesn't come in on Thursdays."

"Oh."

"Is there something I can do to help you?"

"Can you tell me where she lives?"

He shook his head. "I'm sorry, the—"

"Never mind," Quinn cut him off. She started to leave the store, still absentmindedly holding one of the statues.

Almost immediately, the old man was by her side.

"Just what did you think you were doing? I suppose you thought you could get away with stealing? You young people are all alike!"

Quinn looked down at the statue. She realized that she had forgotten to put it down. "I'm sorry. I wasn't stealing. Honest."

"Well, do you want it or not?"

With shaking fingers, Quinn put the figure down. She hurried from the shop. She hoped that the old geezer wouldn't tell Logan and his mother what had happened. She'd just die if he thought she was a thief! She was sorry that she had even mentioned Mrs. James's name. Her heart still hammering, she made her way to the harbor café where she had agreed to meet Ben. She sat down at the same table she had the night before. Was Logan thinking about her now? She hoped so. She picked up the menu.

"What'll it be?"

Quinn glanced up to the waitress. "Coffee, please."

"Anything else?"

Quinn shook her head. She looked out over the horizon. Small clouds sped eastward across the sky and seemed to play tag with the few boats that were out. The gulls swooped down near the pier and stopped momentarily, displaying a particular independence that Quinn wished she had. She inhaled the sweet, salt-scented air.

"This seat taken?"

She looked up to see Logan.

The coffee cup nearly dropped from her hand. "Uh, no." Had he been to the shop?

Did he know she had been there looking for his mom? Did he know about the incident with the old man?

"Had to come into town and deliver some things to the store for Mom."

Quinn's face flushed the color of ripe cranberries. So he did know.

"And I just stopped here for a Coke before going home."

He didn't mention the old man. Quinn decided she wasn't going to say anything, either. She wasn't a thief—no matter what the disagreeable salesman said.

"How are things at home?"

"You mean at the Harris house?"

"Oh, yeah. Right."

"Okay, I guess." Quinn studied him and wondered if he'd be upset if she asked any questions.

"Wait a second. I can see a serious conversation coming on." He grinned and sipped his Coke.

But before he could ask her a question, she saw Ben coming toward them, with a nasty gleam in his eye.

"I want you to stay away from my stepsister, James," he said angrily, towering over Quinn.

Without waiting for Logan's response, he grabbed Quinn's hand. Roughly he pulled her from the chair and dragged her out of the café toward the waiting car. He threw open the door and pushed her inside.

"Ben..." Quinn tried to talk as her stepbrother jumped into the car and pressed the gas pedal. "I don't understand! I was waiting for you, as we agreed!"

"You were talking to Logan James. Mom told you not to speak to him."

"I didn't arrange our meeting. I didn't even know until a few hours ago that Beverly was going to ask you to drive me to town."

"You had time to call him."

"But I didn't."

Furious, he pressed the gas pedal again. They had left Woods Hole behind and now were speeding along the forested road.

"Where are we going?" She watched the leafy trees and bushes rush by in a blur.

"Falmouth. Have to pick up something there. And this time no meeting anyone! Just stay in the car—get it?"

Glancing at her watch, Quinn saw it was almost seven o'clock. Maybe Dad and Bev had gone out, and not told her. Her throat tightened with the prospect. It would be just like her father to do something like that. If they had forgotten to give her instructions about dinner, she'd better go downstairs and get something to eat for herself.

She pushed open the kitchen door and heard something bubbling in a pot on the stove. She went over and lifted the lid. A stew of some kind. It looked gross.

She put the lid back on and lowered the fire.

Where was everyone?

She glanced around the room and saw an open bag of pastries on the table. Why weren't they in the refrigerator? Even she knew that custard creams had to be kept cold.

Standing at the stove, she lifted the cover off the pot again. It really did look terrible. Maybe she would just eat an éclair and that would be her dinner. Four hundred calories was four hundred calories either way, she rationalized.

"Hello, darling. Getting hungry?"

"Oh, hi, Bev. I was curious about dinner."

Beverly shrugged. "We'll eat soon. But if you want, take your dessert now."

"Well, maybe I will take part of it now. If you're sure dinner won't be for a while yet."

"I'm sure, dear. I'm finishing work on this statue and I really have to get it right. I only came in here actually to get more water to wet my clay."

"Thanks."

"You want a plate?"

Quinn shook her head. "It's okay. I'm going to finish it now, anyway. No sense in getting a plate dirty."

Beverly shrugged. "Why don't you go back up to your room, dear? I'll call you when we're ready to eat."

"Okay."

Quinn watched Bev take the water she wanted and leave the kitchen. She thought about going upstairs, but she knew if she did that Alex would beg her for some of the éclair.

Okay, so she was being selfish. Chocolate wasn't good for him, anyway. The vet had told her so.

Taking a napkin and the rest of her dessert, Quinn left the house by the balcony steps. Carefully she made her way down to the beach.

Sitting on the beach, watching the gulls play tag with the clouds and the sails move along the horizon was like being in a world all her own. Lost in a dream, she didn't realize how much time had passed until the sky began to darken. She'd started to leave almost at the same moment she heard the car approaching.

Dizziness washed over her like a hurricane tide. She tried to grab the rail, but missed and stumbled forward. Her foot caught on one of the rocks, preventing her from falling farther.

"Quinn? You all right?" Logan's words echoed in her ears as if through a long tunnel.

She tried to nod, but the black cloud that had surrounded him enveloped her and she closed her eyes.

# Chapter Nine

The first sound she heard was the beeping of the machine over her head. Her arm ached. Quinn looked over to see an intravenous tube attached to her.

In the distance, she could see the white uniforms of the nurse and doctors. What had happened? She recalled finished the éclair, being on the beach and fainting. Logan had been there, hadn't he?

A button hung over her head. She pushed it and saw the light over her head go on.

"Oh, good. You're awake."

Quinn nodded. "Can I have something to drink?"

"I'll check with the doctor. You know, you had a close call there. If you're going to use drugs, you ought to be careful what you're doing."

The nurse disappeared before Quinn could question her. Drugs! There had to be some mistake.

Quinn strained to read the note on her intravenous bottle, but all it had was her name. There was a clipboard at the end of the bed, but try as she would, there was no way to reach it.

"What did you use, Miss Philips, and how much?"

Quinn shook her head, unable to speak.

"We can cure your body momentarily. But we can't do anything further to help you unless you tell us what you were using. Was it cocaine? Heroin?"

To each of them Quinn shook her head. All of this had to be a nightmare. "You're wrong. I haven't used anything."

Finally the nurse pulled the doctor away to talk to another patient. "We'll transfer you to a private room in a few minutes," she told Quinn. "You can rest there."

"Thanks," Quinn said. "I'm fine, though. Why can't I go home?"

"Whatever you took, honey, gave a dreadful shock to your system. You're lucky you're still on this planet. Doctor wants to keep you a couple of days for observation."

"I didn't take anything! I swear it!"

The nurse shrugged and pulled the curtain around Quinn's bed.

What could have happened? Maybe it had been in her coffee at the restaurant? But no, she would have felt the effects earlier.

Could it have been the éclair? Had it been left out too long? Maybe the cream had gone bad and made her ill. The doctors had definitely made a mistake in their diagnosis. After all, doctors weren't infallible, were they?

She thought of Alex. Dad wouldn't think to change his water bowl and feed him. She knew that neither Ben nor Bev would, either.

An hour later, she was moved to a private room on the second floor. Staring mindlessly at the TV, watching one of the soap operas that her mother and she sometimes saw together, Quinn tried to understand the events that had taken place. Something had to have been wrong with the éclair cream. That was the only possible answer.

The knock on her door startled her. "Come in," she called.

A bouquet of flowers appeared first, and then Logan.

"Hi! How you feeling?"

"I'm okay, I guess." Was Logan going to doubt her word, too? "Am I imagining it or did you talk to me on the beach last night?"

"It wasn't last night. It was two nights ago."

She looked at him quizzically.

"You were out cold in intensive care for nearly forty-eight hours."

"Oh. Guess I don't remember."

He handed her the flowers. "Guess you don't. Do you remember anything that happened before?"

"I didn't take anything and I don't do drugs, if that's what you want to know."

Logan looked as if he didn't believe her.

"I don't do drugs. I told you. If they were in my system, well, I don't know how they got in there."

Quinn shook her head. "The only thing I can think of is that something might have been in the éclair. But that's almost as silly as saying I took drugs. I don't know." She paused. "I think maybe you ought to go. I'm kind of tired."

"Yeah, all right. I'll stop in later."

"If you want." She tried to keep her voice even. "Logan," she paused, her throat tight, "I'm worried about Alex. I mean, Dad isn't too careful and…Ben and Bev…" She glanced up at him, pleading.

"I'll go check on the cat. Make sure he's fed."

"Will you? I mean, can you?"

"No problem. There's a way to get up to the house where I won't be bothered."

"A secret passageway?"

"Not really secret. It was used for the Underground Railroad. But no one uses it now. I'm sure Ben and Bev have forgotten about it. Even if they haven't, they won't bother me. I'll take care of Alex and then leave."

"I'd appreciate it. Thank you."

"My pleasure."

She could tell by the tone that he meant well. At least she had one friend here—two, if she counted Alexander.

She didn't know if she could stand being here two more days. She had a mystery to solve.

"Quinn! What are you doing here this time of night?" Mrs. James opened the door to let her in. "Did someone bring you? Is something wrong?"

This was the first time Quinn had ventured out since her release from the hospital but she'd had to see Logan. "Is Logan at home?" she asked.

"No, darling. He's out. But come have a cup of tea with me. He'll be back shortly, and then I'll have him drive you back. There was a time when one could be out at all hours in these woods and never worry, but today you have to be careful. I don't think it's right to have you riding your bike in the dark. And you just out of the hospital, too."

"Well, I . . ."

"Come in and have some tea," Mrs. James urged. "We should call your father, too. I'll bet he's worried you're not back yet."

"I'll bet he doesn't even realize I'm gone."

"That's silly. How can your father not realize you're not home?"

"You don't know my dad."

"Well, let's have the tea and talk a bit. We can call later."

Quinn sat down on the comfortable cushioned rocker and stared into the fire that had just been started. The inside of the Jameses' cottage was nothing like the outside. Despite the worn effect, it had a homey atmosphere of polished wood floors, rag rugs and Early American pine furniture with doilies on the headrests. There was a warmth here that was lacking at the Harris house.

"I hope you're feeling better." Mrs. James carried the tea in on a tray.

"Much, thank you. I think someone tried to play a nasty trick on me."

"Trick, dear?"

"Well, I certainly didn't take drugs the way everyone is saying I did. Maybe it was ptomaine poisoning or some virus."

Mrs. James looked thoughtful. "Do you think that Ben could be involved in drugs? After all, his own father, my brother, died because of them."

Quinn stared at her. "You're related to Bev and Ben?"

The turn of the doorknob stopped Mrs. James from answering. "That you, darling? We have a guest."

"Quinn? What are you doing here? I thought I recognized Ben's bike, but couldn't think of why he'd be here, especially on a bike!" He smiled and shook his head.

"I didn't know you were Ben's cousin."

Logan seemed to be taken aback. "Yes, I am."

"Why don't you two get along?"

"You'll have to ask him that." His hand was on the doorknob. "Truck's still warm. You want a ride back with your bike? Not a good thing to be in the woods at night.''

"Perhaps you'd better get going, darling. That hospitalization must've been a shock to your system. I'd suggest you get to bed early." Mrs. James patted Quinn's hand. "You'll be in Woods Hole for a while yet. We can chat later."

Logan held the door open for her.

She watched as he lifted her bike into the back of the truck.

The oppressive silence as they started back to Route 6 was like the classroom when the teacher passed out the finals. Quinn knew she shouldn't be asking so many questions, but she had to know.

"Your mom said that her brother was Ben's father."

"Right."

She waited a moment, but he didn't volunteer any more.

"She also started to say something about him dying from an overdose."

"You could say that." He shifted gears to let another car pass.

"Aren't you going to tell me?"

"I don't really think you should know."

"And I think I should." She turned to him. "I told you, Logan, I didn't take that drug. Why doesn't anyone believe me?"

Logan reached out and touched her shoulder. "I do believe you. But drop it."

"If you won't tell me, I'll ask Bev."

Logan laughed. "I doubt she'll tell anything."

Quinn folded her arms and peered out onto the road. She glanced at Logan. Where was he taking her? "We are going back to Dad's, aren't we?"

"Sure. Why? You have someplace else you need to go?"

She shook her head. "I just don't recognize the way."

"Back roads."

It was nearly five minutes more before she realized he was right.

Just below the house, he pulled the truck over. "I don't think it's a good idea for me to drive you all the way up. Why don't we take your bike out now? I can watch you."

She hopped out of the truck and took the bike from him. "Thanks for the ride."

"You're welcome."

"And thanks for taking care of Alex. I saw his water bowl had been filled."

Logan shrugged. "I only got in once when Ben and Bev were out. I would have gone more but..."

She nodded. "I understand." Her leg went over the bike. "Do you think you'll show me the secret passage one day? It would be fun to explore before I leave."

"Sure."

He was waiting for her to get into the house. She'd have to talk to him some other time. Pumping her leg down, she started to bike up the road.

# Chapter Ten

Quinn wasn't sure if Alex had woken her when he moved, or if she'd heard something. Maybe both. His ears were straight up and his whole body alert as his eyes scanned the room. She did the same. But all she could hear were the waves. She looked at the clock. Two-thirty!

"What is it, boy? What's wrong, Alex?"

He pawed at the blanket as he tried to get her up.

"All right. All right." Quinn threw back the covers. "No, you are not going out. I've told you that before."

Alex looked at her with pleading eyes. She picked him up. "Be a good cat and let me sleep. I've been through a lot and I'm tired."

He laid his head against the crook of her arm, but a moment later decided he had had enough and jumped down.

Back at the door, he began scratching again.

"Alex, there is nothing out there for you." She picked him up once more and this time opened the door. Only the shadows of the night. A dim light in the main hall downstairs flickered. Dad was probably staying over in Boston and Ben was probably still out somewhere. "See?" She held the cat up so he could look down the empty hall. The action was as much for her benefit as for his.

"Let's go back to sleep. Okay?"

Nearly a half hour went by. She should have been able to fall back to sleep, but so far sleep had eluded her. Still lying awake thinking, Quinn stared at the door.

*The handle was moving.*

Blood rushed through her ears, pounding like angry surf in a storm. "Hello?"

The movement of the handle stopped. "Dad, is that you?"

"Dad?" She got up and opened the door.

The hall was empty.

"More pancakes, Quinn?" Bev asked.

"No, thanks." Quinn pushed her plate away.

"You haven't eaten much, dear. Are you still feeling ill?"

"She must be," Ben said. "And I'm not surprised. I can think of far better ways to use the stuff, kid. I mean, if you're going to use it."

"I don't use it."

He smiled knowingly at her, before draining his coffee cup.

When Ben had sauntered out, Quinn asked, "Dad coming back today?"

"Do you want me to call the university and find out?"

"No, that's all right."

"Something special you want to talk to him about?"

"Just things. It can wait."

"I'm a good listener."

"Thought you had work to finish up for your show. Those masks must take a lot of time to make."

Beverly smiled and touched Quinn's arm. "I do, but, darling, you are David's daughter and I really haven't had much time to get to know you. Maybe you'd like to see Nantucket Island. It's a lovely place to visit for the day. We can go there tomorrow—all four of us—you, me, Ben and Dave. We'll be a real family. Won't that be nice?"

"Yeah." Quinn drank the rest of her coffee. It was as bitter as the last time.

"You're going to read on the beach today, aren't you?"

"I guess so. Don't have any other plans unless Dad gets home."

Bev nodded. "Just don't go wandering off the way you did yesterday, honey. I like to know where you are."

Back in the bedroom, Quinn searched for her bathing suit. Only as she was headed downstairs did she realize she had forgotten suntan oil.

Rapping on Beverly's studio door, she called out, "Beverly?"

The door was flung open. "What!"

"I'm sorry if I'm bothering you. I need some suntan oil. Do you have any?"

"Look in the bathroom near the study. There should be some there."

The door slammed closed before Quinn could respond.

Sitting on the beach without any company wasn't as much fun as Quinn had hoped. No one was in sight and yet she had the feeling that someone was watching her. Shielding her eyes, Quinn looked back up at the house. Sun glinted against the line of windows, making the building look as if it had an evil smile.

She forced her attention back to the novel she was reading. Even with the book to keep her company and the transistor radio, she felt sad, and very much alone. The tide was coming up and lapping at her toes. Time to move the blanket farther up onto the rock. Suddenly she felt awfully tired. It was tempting to think of falling asleep, but she had been sunburned too many times. Besides, she wanted to be active. She decided to pick up some of the driftwood pieces and shells. Maybe Mrs. James could use what she collected. Maybe she'd even pay something. Certainly the allowance her mother had given her wasn't going to last long, and she didn't see her father enough to ask him for more money.

She picked up the two pieces in front of her, emptied her book bag and placed them in there. Leaving her towel and things on the rocky ledge, Quinn began to walk down the isolated coast, picking up items as she found them.

A rocky wall loomed before her. Several gulls swooped over the water. With the cry of a successful attacker, one of them flew down and grabbed a silvery fish from the water. He flew toward the rock but instead of landing nearby so Quinn could watch him, he flew inside. Quinn realized this was the mouth of a cave.

Entering it was harder than she'd thought it would be. There were two small holes, one at water level and one way above. The one where the bird had gone was too high for her to climb up to. She'd have to go out into the tide and swim to the other one.

Salty water seeped into her mouth, and the sound of the waves echoed in her ears. Grabbing the rocky ledge already underwater, she managed to guide herself inside. She was gasping for breath as she surfaced in the huge dome of the cave.

Holding on to the wall for support, she blinked her eyes. Light was coming in from the hole at the top. Quinn edged around the wall and stared at the tunnel in front of her.

A cool wind gave her goose bumps the size of blueberries. Rocks bit into her bare feet. There were steps in the worn rock. Quinn continued to grope her way along and stepped on something uneven. She winced and picked it up, thinking it might be another shell for the collection.

In the dim light, she saw the black stripe painted across the material. It looked like a piece from one of Beverly's masks. But what would it be doing here hidden in this cave?

She looked again toward the passage, which was darker than night. She thought she should attempt to explore now, but without a light source exploring wasn't going to do much good. No, she would just have to wait until tomorrow.

Already tired from her morning on the beach and her dive under, she had to make an effort to struggle against the water, which seemed to be pressing her back down and away.

With each stroke forward, she seemed to float two strokes back. Was she ever going to get back to shore? The coming wave threatened to swamp her. Quinn knew if she couldn't get hold of the rocky wall and stay there, she might be pulled into the ocean currents. Why had she been so impulsive? She should have waited until low tide to investigate.

Finally she felt her feet touching the firm ground. She didn't want to look back. On dry land, she ran toward the ledge where she had left her blanket, book and radio. The driftwood she had so painstakingly collected was floating out to sea. Gathering up what she could rescue, she hurried toward the rickety steps leading back to the house.

She was surprised to see Logan waiting for her at the top of the incline. "Did you see me down there? I could have drowned. Why didn't you come help me?"

"I just spotted you and I was on my way."

"I found a cave down there."

"Stay away from there, Quinn. It won't do you any good."

"Why? What do you mean? Do those tunnels lead to the house? Were they part of the Underground Railroad?"

"How would I know?"

"Then how did you get in the house to care for Alex?"

Her hands went to her hips as the towel dropped to her feet and along with it the piece of painted clay she had found in the cave. Quinn hadn't realized she still had it in her hand.

"Where did you get that?" he asked.

"Inside the cave. Why?" She paused. "You haven't answered my questions."

"I didn't use the tunnels. I had an old key. Ben gave it to me several years ago and never asked for it back."

She looked up at the house. The sun was shining on the lower windows now, but it still looked as if it were smiling malevolently at her. Was Logan the one who'd been watching her? Or was it someone else? "There was someone in the hall last night. It wasn't my father and I don't think it was Ben."

"Did you ask Bev?"

She shook her head. "It sounded like a man's steps."

Logan frowned. "You sure you weren't dreaming?"

"Positive. I'm going into the house to get lunch. Will you be out here later?"

"Don't know. Maybe. Tide doesn't go out for a while yet."

"Yeah, I guessed. I almost got caught in it."

"Bev didn't tell you the tide schedule?"

"Guess she was too busy with preparing her things for the art show."

Logan shrugged. "You're probably right. But the schedule is printed in the paper each morning. Check it next time you want to go sunbathing."

Quinn started up the stairs and carefully edged into her room so as not to spill the milk or let Alex escape.

"Here, boy," she called when the door had closed firmly behind her. "Here, Alex."

She looked around the room. He wasn't on the bed, the chair or the rug. She put the milk down and went to the window ledge. Not there, either.

"Alex? Where are you hiding?"

She started along the upstairs corridor softly calling his name at each door. She hurried down the stairs. From a distance she could hear Alex crying. "Alex!" She called loudly in the kitchen. She heard soft mewing.

"Where are you?"

He cried again.

"Alex." She stepped into the hall. Her stepmother didn't seem to be around at the moment. Well, that was all right with her. Quinn didn't want Bev to know what mischief Alex had gotten into.

Finally she traced him to a hidden door tucked behind the first floor hall.

Now how in the world had he gotten there? She turned the handle.

It was locked.

"Alex, you okay?"

Quinn tried the handle once more. It wouldn't budge.

She would have to find the key.

## Chapter Eleven

Quinn hated going into her dad's bedroom but she had searched all over and not found the key. She had no choice. She had to get Alex out from behind that locked door. She found the set of keys on Beverly's ruffled vanity. She supposed this unknown room was really none of her business. Nevertheless, she couldn't help being curious. Maybe she'd ask her father about it later.

Meanwhile, she had to free poor Alex.

If Bev had so much work to prepare for her show, why wasn't she at home working?

Well, that wasn't her problem. She opened the door for Alex.

The cat jumped into her arms, licking Quinn's face.

"Hey, what's all this white powder over you? I hope you haven't ruined any of Beverly's plaster masks. She'll kill me if you do."

The cat continued to wash her face with his tongue.

"Come on. Let's see what damage you've done, Alex. Maybe I can fix it before Bev gets back," Quinn said, slipping into the room.

Nothing seemed amiss. Quinn turned her attention to the closet. She opened the door and was surprised to find ascending stairs. Was this the secret passage?

Placing Alex carefully on her shoulder, she slowly began to climb them.

For the second time that day, she wished she had some light.

Noise from below told her that someone was home. Was it Beverly, Ben or her dad?

The top of the stairs had a second door. It was locked. Once again, Quinn fumbled with the keys. Trying to be as quiet as she could she tried one in the lock. To her amazement, she found herself in her bedroom closet! So that was why Alex had been clawing at her closet door that first night! Perhaps someone had climbed up the stairs to her bedroom—but who?

A knock on her door startled her. "Yes?" Quinn hid the keys under her robe.

"Quinn, darling, are you all right?" It was Bev.

"I'm...I'm fine. Just came up from the beach and I'm resting."

"Thank goodness you didn't get caught in the tides. I forgot to warn you about them this morning."

"Oh, no. Everything's fine." The footsteps moved away.

The sound of the car driving up drew Quinn to the window. Her father was home! She heard Bev going downstairs to meet him. Quickly she ran across the hall to the other room, replacing the keys where she had found them.

"Well, princess, how you feeling?"

Quinn shrugged. "Okay, I guess."

"Sorry I haven't been around much. But duty calls. You know how it is."

"Yeah, I guess I do. Dad, why did you even want me out here this summer, anyway? You haven't spent a whole hour with me since I've come."

"Darling, I'm trying. Really I am. Anyway, it was Beverly's idea you spend time with us, too. She wanted to get to know you. I think you and she have developed a good relationship."

They had? Is that what Beverly had told him?

"Dad, I've got to talk to you," she said urgently.

"Is this about the drugs you took?"

"I did not take any drugs! Daddy, I told you. You can ask Mom. You can ask my friends. I don't do drugs. I've never even had any desire for them. In fact, the kids at school tease me for being so straight."

"So how did they get into your system? They didn't magically appear."

Quinn paused and walked to the door. Opening it quickly, she peered into the hallway. She had the feeling that Beverly or Ben might be listening to her conversation with her father.

"Something bothering you, Quinn?"

"Yeah. This place. Something weird is going on in this house. There are tunnels all over the place. A secret door leads into my bedroom from downstairs. There was someone in my room the first night and Alex scared him away. Whoever it was escaped into the closet tunnel."

His look told her that he didn't believe this any more than he believed her about the drugs.

"I'm telling you the truth. If you don't believe me, ask Bev."

"Quinn, have you ever considered a career as a writer? You've got a great imagination, baby."

"Ask Beverly. She can't deny it. I just saw them."

"I'll do that," he said.

The tide was already receding. Quinn ran down to the water's edge and looked for Logan, but he had gone.

There was no one at the cottage, either.

For a brief moment, she thought of going to the sheriff, but what could she report? She had no evidence of any crimes.

Tomorrow she'd find proof of something in the caves. Then her father and Logan had to believe her.

Quinn bicycled back to the old house and headed for her bedroom.

Alex was curled up on the bed in the same position he'd been when she left.

"Hey! You want dinner, Alex?"

"Alex?" Quinn crossed the room to her cat. "Alex?" She stared at the black furry body. His chest wasn't moving and his eyes were open and glassy. "Alex!" She took the cat. He remained motionless.

She grabbed him off the bed and, cuddling him to her, ran down the stairs. "Dad! Dad! Get your car! Hurry, please! Alex's ill!"

Her father came rushing out of his study, Beverly behind him. "What are you shouting about, Quinn?"

"Dad, please. It's Alex. We have to get him to the vet. We have to get him to town. He must have eaten something. He must..."

Her father pried the animal from her and put his fingers to the cat's neck.

"Quinn, I'm sorry. There isn't any pulse. Your cat's dead."

"No! He can't be. Not Alex!" She grabbed the lifeless body from her father. "You did something to him, Beverly!"

"Quinn, really!" her father said.

"Well, it's true! She hated Alex! She must have done something to him!"

"No, Quinn. I didn't touch your cat."

"Well, someone did. He was fine this morning when I found him in your storage room. He was fine until I left to go riding just now."

"Your cat was in the storage room? How did he get there?"

Quinn could barely speak for grief. "The tunnel—he found it. You killed him because of that, didn't you?'' She began sobbing. He had been such a good cat. He hadn't even complained about being shut in her room. ''Oh, Alex!'' She hugged him to her, rocking as she cried.

She was aware of Beverly glancing at her father and of her dad's arm coming around her.

''Dad, she did something to him! I know!''

''Now, baby, it's possible your cat was ill for a long time and we didn't know it. When was the last time he was checked by the vet?''

''Before I brought him out here. He was fine. There was nothing wrong with him. Daddy, she killed him. I know it. He must have found something and...''

''Quinn, I want to hear no more talk about that! I'll buy you a new kitten if you want.''

## Chapter Twelve

Quinn was up early the following morning before anyone in the house had stirred.

Actually she had slept very little the night before. Her dreams, what few times she closed her eyes, had been haunted by visions of Alex. Quinn had never known death before. The raw wound of Alex's death hurt. To think she'd never see Alex again, never feel his soft presence next to her, nudging her awake for school, demanding that she feed him and eating her chocolate grahams. She wiped the tears from her eyes. She would find out what happened to him—and see the person responsible for his death suffer.

Quietly she reached the first floor. So far so good.

On the bike, she pedaled furiously in the reddish dawn to Logan's house. He had to be home now, she thought. He had to help her! He was the only one she could think of who would understand. Quinn realized that she was no longer scared for herself. When someone attacked a helpless animal—well, that made her hackles rise!

There was no smoke coming from the cottage chimney. Maybe they weren't up yet. She didn't think they would have left this early, but what did she really know about Logan and his mother? Logan had told her about the tunnels. Did that mean he knew why they were being used? Even if she brought proof to her father, she wondered if he would believe her or if he would continue to believe Beverly.

Clasping her arms around her knees, Quinn sat on the porch of the cottage and wondered what to do. If she didn't go back now, Beverly and Ben would probably cause a fuss. Besides, she told herself, she didn't know for sure that anything was really going on. With a sigh, she climbed on the bike and pedaled back to the house.

"Quinn! Quinn!"

Quinn turned to see her father calling. He was motioning to her.

"Your mom's on the phone. Come talk to her."

Eagerly, she ran up the path, taking the steps two at a time.

She took the call in her father's study.

"Mom, hi!"

The crackling noise on the other end told her that her mother was still overseas. "Is something the matter?"

"No, darling. We're having a good time. I just called to see how you were getting on with your father."

"Oh. I'm doing fine." She wanted to pour out all her troubles and worries to her mother, but what could Mom do so far away.

"Your father told me about Alexander. I'm sorry, honey. I know how much you loved the cat."

"Yeah." The torrent of tears threatened to wash over her again. Because she knew the cat had loved her, losing Alex felt worse than when Mom had told her Dad was leaving them.

Her father was on the other side of the room. He was watching her, but he didn't seem to be listening. Quinn wondered if she should tell Mom what she feared about Alex's death. "Mom, I..." Quinn heard a noise, like a breathing sound, and paused. Was someone listening in? "Mom, I miss you. Come home soon."

"I will, baby. Your father says there's a great school on the Cape for you."

"No, I want to be home with you!" She looked over at her father. Her words had been loud enough for him to hear. "Listen, I gotta go. This is costing you a fortune. Give my love to Paul."

"Sure, sweetheart. Put Daddy back on the line."

"Come on, Quinn. Hurry up. It's time to go." Beverly was getting impatient.

"You're sure Dad's meeting us at the docks?"

"Of course. He wouldn't miss this trip."

"Okay. Let me just run upstairs for my sweater."

Quinn didn't want to go to Nantucket on this outing. Especially since her father wasn't here. He'd been acting preoccupied since last night when Logan had come to see him. They'd spent over an hour in her dad's study, then Logan had left, without so much as a word to her. And her dad had gone out early this morning, before breakfast even. Was something going on?

"Quinn!"

She couldn't stall any longer. Walking slowly, she joined Bev and Ben by the Porsche.

"Couldn't we wait just a few more minutes?" she pleaded. "Where is Dad anyway?"

"Something came up at the university. Don't worry, darling. He'll be following us."

"Seems kind of silly to take two cars."

Beverly opened the car door for her. "No, it doesn't, Quinn. Ben will probably want his car when we return, so it's just as well."

"Right. I will." Her stepbrother grinned as Quinn reluctantly took the seat.

The car shot off with lightning speed.

At the docks, Beverly directed Quinn toward the small motorboat at the end of the pier.

"Aren't we taking the ferry?" she asked, looking at the large ship that carried the day trippers back and forth to Nantucket and Martha's Vineyard.

"No, I thought it would be fun if we rented our own boat, honey."

"Oh. Fine."

"Why don't you look at the boat while we wait for your father?"

Quinn nodded and went on board. There wasn't much space on deck, but the cabin inside was roomier than she expected it to be. It even had a refrigerator, cooking area and two beds.

She lifted the hatch to look down and noticed several crates piled against the wall. One of Beverly's African masks lay on top of them.

Quinn hoisted herself up. Suddenly she didn't want to take a trip to Nantucket. She didn't want to go anywhere with her stepmother and stepbrother.

Before she could get to the main deck, however, she heard the motor turn over. She felt the boat lurch as it started out to sea. Quinn grabbed the railing and managed to reach the main deck. She saw Beverly staring out to sea and Ben steering.

"My dad here?"

Beverly shook her head. "No, he said he was going to be tied up today. The university needed him."

"When did he contact you? We've only been here a short time."

They were cutting through the churning water at breakneck speed, creating high, cresting waves on either side. Already the shore was becoming distant.

"He called in at the station when I was making final arrangements for the boat."

"But my dad . . . ?"

"Is fine, Quinn," Beverly said soothingly. "You want some milk and brownies? I know you didn't eat much breakfast."

"No, thanks. I'm not hungry." She stared back forlornly at the frothing wake.

The motor slowed. Quinn shielded her eyes and looked up to her stepbrother. "Why are we stopping?"

"Probably out of gas." Ben climbed down as Beverly went below.

"How can we be out of gas? Didn't you check that before we left?"

"Guess I forgot." Leaning against the rail, he squinted up at the sun.

"Aren't you going to check on it?"

"Sure. In a minute." Ben smiled at her. He poured a glass of milk and handed it to her.

"I told your mom, I'm not hungry."

"A shame. It would make things easier."

"What's easier?"

He didn't answer. "I'm sorry about your cat, Quinn. I wasn't crazy about the creature, but I don't like death." He paused and picked up a glazed sweet. "It's too bad you brought him here in the first place. I don't think you would have noticed me the first night if it hadn't been for him.''

Quinn's eyes went wide. "It was you in my room?''

Ben nodded. "Both times. I tried to give you some easy outs, but you didn't take them. If you had eaten the whole English muffin that first day..."

"When my dad got sick, you mean?''

"We didn't mean for Dave to become ill. Though you understand he'll have to be done away with eventually, too.''

Quinn stared at him blankly. "Done away with? You mean you're going to kill my father?''

"After we take care of you, of course.'' He paused. His tone was as light as if he were just telling her she had won a scholarship to Northwestern. "It makes sense to do you in first. You see, by the terms of the will, as your father's only heir, you'd get all his money if anything happened to him. Well, once you're gone, Mom and I would get the money.''

Quinn couldn't believe she was hearing these things. She felt frozen, unable to move or think.

"I wasn't imagining things, then," she stammered.

He grinned. "You're a pretty intelligent kid. If your death wasn't so critical, I'd ask you to join the operation. But you see, I lost so much dope in the last raid that getting money from your father is the only way I can make it up. And if I don't—well, you can imagine what'll happen to me. Guys in this business play rough."

"Then there was something in the éclair..."

"I thought that was pretty neat. Mom didn't like the idea so much, but your father had told us that you had a sweet tooth, so..."

"My dad—did my dad have any inkling that you and your mother were dealing in drugs?"

"Oh, Mom's not a real dealer. She just lets me use her masks to hide the stuff in. She doesn't have any choice. Mom's got her pride, you see. My own father died in a drug bust. He was a runner, like me. Our house is perfect for the operation, on the coast, with the tunnels and all. Dad brought me in on the business. Mom didn't want anyone to know. More than that, she doesn't want anything to happen to her baby boy, and she knows what my buddies will do to me if I don't come up with some cash soon. Why do you think she married your old man?"

Quinn's brain was working again. "But people do know about you. I mean, Logan said . . ."

"What did my cousin say?"

Quinn backed away from the fury in Ben's face, and the rail pressed against her spine. The numbness was melting away, and she began to feel sheer terror.

"He told me about your father. He suspects you." She had never been a good liar. She only hoped that Ben believed her and that it would help her somehow.

"I want to know exactly what he said." He approached menacingly.

"You know you'll never get away with this. My dad will find out. In fact, Dad already knows about the powder in the masks. I showed it to him the other day."

Ben started to laugh. "Oh, no, you didn't, Quinn. Besides, he would never believe you. He doesn't want to believe any wrong of Beverly or me. She has him charmed."

Suddenly he reached for her, grabbing her arm and twisting it behind her back. In a quick movement, he had flipped her over the rail. She felt herself sinking in the freezing water, but by flailing her arms, she managed to surface. She gasped for air and tried to tread water.

At first she thought the sounds she heard were just the waves rushing by her and the blood pulsating through her brain. But when Quinn looked up she saw a helicopter. Then, astonishingly, she heard her father's voice over a loudspeaker. "Give up, Ben. That's a Coast Guard boat behind you."

Ben responded by revving the boat's engine, but before he could take off, the Coast Guard cutter had pulled alongside.

"Hey! Hey! What about me?" Quinn waved frantically.

The helicopter hovered as someone dropped her a lifeline.

Through the haze of bright sun reflected off water, Quinn could just make out two familiar faces peering down at her. *Her father and Logan.* As she was drawn closer, she could see the tears in her father's eyes, and she felt a fierce surge of love for him. He might not be a perfect father—he would probably always be preoccupied and too busy for her—but he did love her and he would be there for her when she needed him.

"Don't leave without me next time," he said in a choked voice as his arms reached out to pull Quinn into the helicopter.

"Yeah," Logan added. "If anybody is going to take you for a ride, it'd better be me."

Quinn gave him a shaky smile. She was safe. This summer's storm had passed and she could see wonderful clear days ahead.

| QUANTITY | BOOK # | ISBN # | TITLE | AUTHOR | PRICE |
|---|---|---|---|---|---|
| ☐ | 129 | 06129-3 | The Ghost of Gamma Rho | Elaine Harper | $1.95 |
| ☐ | 130 | 06130-7 | Nightshade | Jesse Osborne | 1.95 |
| ☐ | 131 | 06131-5 | Waiting for Amanda | Cheryl Zach | 1.95 |
| ☐ | 132 | 06132-3 | The Candy Papers | Helen Cavanagh | 1.95 |
| ☐ | 133 | 06133-1 | Manhattan Melody | Marilyn Youngblood | 1.95 |
| ☐ | 134 | 06134-X | Killebrew's Daughter | Janice Harrell | 1.95 |
| ☐ | 135 | 06135-8 | Bid for Romance | Dorothy Francis | 1.95 |
| ☐ | 136 | 06136-6 | The Shadow Knows | Becky Stewart | 1.95 |
| ☐ | 137 | 06137-4 | Lover's Lake | Elaine Harper | 1.95 |
| ☐ | 138 | 06138-2 | In the Money | Beverly Sommers | 1.95 |
| ☐ | 139 | 06139-0 | Breaking Away | Josephine Wunsch | 1.95 |
| ☐ | 140 | 06140-4 | What I Know About Boys | McClure Jones | 1.95 |
| ☐ | 141 | 06141-2 | I Love You More Than Chocolate | Frances Hurley Grimes | 1.95 |
| ☐ | 142 | 06142-0 | The Wilder Special | Rose Bayner | 1.95 |
| ☐ | 143 | 06143-9 | Hungarian Rhapsody | Marilyn Youngblood | 1.95 |
| ☐ | 144 | 06144-7 | Country Boy | Joyce McGill | 1.95 |
| ☐ | 145 | 06145-5 | Janine | Elaine Harper | 1.95 |
| ☐ | 146 | 06146-3 | Call Back Yesterday | Doreen Owens Malek | 1.95 |
| ☐ | 147 | 06147-1 | Why Me? | Beverly Sommers | 1.95 |
| ☐ | 149 | 06149-8 | Off the Hook | Rose Bayner | 1.95 |
| ☐ | 150 | 06150-1 | The Heartbreak of Haltom High | Dawn Kingsbury | 1.95 |
| ☐ | 151 | 06151-X | Against the Odds | Andrea Marshall | 1.95 |
| ☐ | 152 | 06152-8 | On the Road Again | Miriam Morton | 1.95 |
| ☐ | 159 | 06159-5 | Sugar 'n' Spice | Janice Harrell | 1.95 |
| ☐ | 160 | 06160-9 | The Other Langley Girl | Joyce McGill | 1.95 |

Your Order Total $ _____

☐ (Minimum 2 Book Order)
New York and Arizona residents
add appropriate sales tax $ _____

Postage and Handling _____ .75

I enclose _____

Name _____

Address _____

City _____

State/Prov. _____ Zip/Postal Code _____

FL-RO-2

# First Love from Silhouette

### DON'T MISS THESE FOUR TITLES— AVAILABLE THIS MONTH . . .

---

## GHOST SHIP Becky Stuart
### A Kellogg and Carey Story

One stormy night, Carey spotted a ship tossing and heaving off the Long Island shore. No one believed her. Now it was up to Kellogg and Theodore to establish her credibility.

## A GATHERING STORM Serita Stevens

Spending the summer with her absentminded father and his disagreeable new family in his spooky old house turned out to be a frightening experience for Quinn. Fortunately she had two loyal friends, her beloved cat and Logan, a local boy, determined to protect her.

## WHEELS Rebecca Nunn

Robin was sure that three was a crowd when she suspected that her best friend was seeing Keith, her first real boyfriend. How would she ever cope with such a betrayal?

## FIRST IMPRESSIONS
### Kalindi Clare

Kira was dazzled by Stav from the first moment that she saw him in art class. Had she grasped the whole picture, or was she losing her sense of perspective?

# WATCH FOR THESE TITLES FROM FIRST LOVE COMING NEXT MONTH

---

### ROAD TO ROMANCE A Hart Mystery!
### Nicole Hart

When Angelica and her friends took a guided tour through Italy, they discovered that it was definitely the setting for romance and intrigue—and maybe even murder.

### PROMISES
### Tracy West

For four long years Carlie had been separated from her childhood chum, Gordie. Now he was coming home. Could they pick up where they had left off, or would she be greeting a total stranger?

### THE ROAR OF THE CROWD
### Alan Thomas

When Trevor reluctantly agreed to his father's suggestion that he join the school football team, he hoped to take the offensive with the prettiest cheerleader, Allison. He only hoped that if he tackled her, she would not block his pass.

### NONE BUT THE BRAVE
### Hazel Krantz

For the first time in her life Kelly was in love. It was a love deeper and more compelling than she had ever imagined was possible. Did Dennis feel the same way?

*First Love from Silhouette*